"What does anything matter, when I know—that the end is near!"

THE NOVELS AND STORIES OF
RICHARD HARDING DAVIS

THE WHITE MICE

BY

RICHARD HARDING DAVIS

WITH AN INTRODUCTION BY

JOHN FOX, Jr.

ILLUSTRATED

NEW YORK
CHARLES SCRIBNER'S SONS
1927

COPYRIGHT, 1909, 1916, 1920, BY
CHARLES SCRIBNER'S SONS

Printed in the United States of America

RICHARD HARDING DAVIS

During the twenty years that I knew him Richard Harding Davis was always going to some far-off land. He was just back from a trip somewhere when I first saw him in his rooms in New York, rifle in hand, in his sock feet and with his traps in confusion about him. He was youth incarnate—ruddy, joyous, vigorous, adventurous, self-confident youth—and, in all the years since, that first picture of him has suffered no change with me. He was so intensely alive that I cannot think of him as dead—and I do not. He is just away on another of those trips and it really seems queer that I shall not hear him tell about it.

We were together as correspondents in the Spanish War and in the Russo-Japanese War we were together again; and so there is hardly any angle from which I have not had the chance to know him. No man was ever more misunderstood by those who did not know him or better understood by those who knew him well, for he carried nothing in the back of his head—no card that was not face up on the table. Every thought, idea, purpose, principle within him was for the world to read and to those who could not know how rigidly he matched his inner and outer life he was almost unbelievable. He was exacting in friendship because his standard was high and because he gave what he asked; and if he told you of a fault he told you first of a virtue that made the fault seem small indeed. But he told you and expected you to tell him.

Naturally, the indirection of the Japanese was incomprehensible to him. He was not good at picking up strange tongues and the Japanese equivalent for the Saxon monosyllable for what the Japanese was to him he never learned. For only one other word did he have more use and I believe it was the only one he knew, "hyaku—hurry!" Over there I was in constant fear for him because of his knight-errancy and his candor. Once he came near being involved in a duel because of his quixotic championship of a woman whom he barely knew, and disliked, and whose absent husband he did not know at all. And more than once I looked for a Japanese to draw his two-handed ancestral sword when Dick bluntly demanded a reconciliation of his yea of yesterday with his nay of to-day. Nine months passed and we never heard the whistle of bullet or shell. Dick called himself a "cherry-blossom correspondent," and when our ship left those shores each knew that the other went to his state-room and in bitter chagrin and disappointment wept quite childishly.

RICHARD HARDING DAVIS

Of course, he was courageous—absurdly so—and, in spite of his high-strung temperament, always calm and cool. At El Paso hill, the day after the fight, the rest of us scurried for tree-trunks when a few bullets whistled near; but Dick stalked out in the open and with his field-glasses searched for the supposed sharpshooters in the trees. Lying under a bomb-proof when the Fourth of July bombardment started, I saw Dick going unhurriedly down the hill for his glasses, which he had left in Colonel Roosevelt's tent, and unhurriedly going back up to the trenches again. Under the circumstances I should have been content with my naked eye. A bullet thudded close to where Dick lay with a soldier.

"That hit you?" asked Dick. The soldier grunted "No," looked sidewise at Dick, and muttered an oath of surprise. Dick had not taken his glasses from his eyes. I saw him writhing on the ground with sciatica during that campaign, like a snake, but pulling his twisted figure straight and his tortured face into a smile if a soldier or stranger passed.

He was easily the first reporter of his time—perhaps of all time. Out of any incident or situation he could pick the most details that would interest the most people and put them in a way that was pleasing to the most people; and always, it seemed, he had the extraordinary good judgment or the

RICHARD HARDING DAVIS

extraordinary good luck to be just where the most interesting thing was taking place.

Gouverneur Morris has written the last word about Richard Harding Davis, and he, as every one must, laid final stress on the clean body, clean heart, and clean mind of the man. R. H. D. never wrote a line that cannot be given to his little daughter when she is old enough to read, and I never heard a word pass his lips that his own mother could not hear. There are many women in the world like the women in his books. There are a few men like the men, and of these Dick himself was one.

JOHN FOX, JR.

ILLUSTRATIONS

"WHAT DOES ANYTHING MATTER, WHEN I KNOW—THAT THE END IS NEAR!" *Frontispiece*

                                                FACING PAGE

UNDER THE BLOW THE MASKED MAN STAGGERED DRUNKENLY 70

SHIFTING THE REINS TO HIS LEFT HAND, RODDY LET THE OTHER FALL UPON HIS REVOLVER 112

"NOW I KNOW . . . WHY I CAME TO VENEZUELA" 144

ON SUCH A NIGHT . . . LEANDER SWAM THE HELLESPONT 192

HER FINGERS TRACED THE SIGN OF THE CROSS 292

THE WHITE MICE

I

ONCE upon a time a lion dropped his paw upon a mouse.

"Please let me live!" begged the mouse, "and some day I will do as much for you."

"That is so funny," roared the king of beasts, "that we will release you. We had no idea mice had a sense of humor."

And then, as you remember, the lion was caught in the net of the hunter, and struggled, and fought, and struck blindly, until his spirit and strength were broken, and he lay helpless and dying.

And the mouse, happening to pass that way, gnawed and nibbled at the net, and gave the lion his life.

The morals are: that an appreciation of humor is a precious thing; that God moves in a mysterious way, His wonders to perform, and that you never can tell.

In regard to this fable it is urged that, according to the doctrine of chances, it is extremely unlikely that at the very moment the lion lay

THE WHITE MICE

bound and helpless the very same mouse should pass by. But the explanation is very simple and bromidic.

It is this—that this is a small world.

People who are stay-at-home bodies come to believe the whole world is the village in which they live. People who are rolling-stones claim that if you travel far enough and long enough the whole world becomes as one village; that sooner or later you make friends with every one in it; that the only difference between the stay-at-homes and the gadabouts is that while the former answer local telephone calls, the others receive picture postal-cards. There is a story that seems to illustrate how small this world is. In fact, this is the story.

General Don Miguel Rojas, who as a young man was called the Lion of Valencia, and who later had honorably served Venezuela as Minister of Foreign Affairs, as Secretary of War, as Minister to the Court of St. James and to the Republic of France, having reached the age of sixty found himself in a dungeon-cell underneath the fortress in the harbor of Porto Cabello. He had been there two years. The dungeon was dark and very damp, and at high-tide the waters of the harbor oozed through the pores of the limestone walls. The air was the air of a receiving-vault, and held the odor of a fisherman's creel.

General Rojas sat huddled upon a canvas cot, with a blanket about his throat and a blanket about his knees, reading by the light of a candle the story of Don Quixote. Sometimes a drop of water fell upon the candle and it sputtered, and its light was nearly lost in the darkness. Sometimes so many drops gathered upon the white head of the Lion of Valencia that he sputtered, too, and coughed so violently that, in agony, he beat with feeble hands upon his breast. And *his* light, also, nearly escaped into the darkness.

On the other side of the world, four young Americans, with legs crossed and without their shoes, sat on the mats of the tea-house of the Hundred and One Steps. On their sun-tanned faces was the glare of Yokohama Bay, in their eyes the light of youth, of intelligent interest, of adventure. In the hand of each was a tiny cup of acrid tea. Three of them were under thirty, and each wore the suit of silk pongee that in eighteen hours C. Tom, or Little Ah Sing, the Chinese King, fits to any figure, and which in the Far East is the badge of the tourist tribe. Of the three, one was Rodman Forrester. His father, besides being pointed out as the parent of "Roddy" Forrester, the onetime celebrated Yale pitcher, was himself not unfavorably known to many governments as a constructor of sky-scrapers, breakwaters, bridges, wharves and light-houses, which latter he planted on slippery rocks along inaccessible coast-lines. Among his fellow Captains of Industry he was known as the Forrester Construction Company, or, for short, the "F. C. C." Under that alias Mr. Forrester was now trying to sell to the Japanese three light-houses, to illuminate the Inner Sea between Kobe and Shimoneseki. To hasten the sale he had shipped "Roddy" straight from the machine-shops to Yokohama.

Three years before, when Roddy left Yale, his father ordered him abroad to improve his mind by travel, and to inspect certain light-houses and breakwaters on both shores of the English Channel. While crossing from Dover to Calais on his way to Paris, Roddy made a very superficial survey of the light-houses and reported that, so far as he could see by daylight, they still were on the job. His father, who had his own breezy sense of humor, cancelled Roddy's letter of credit, cabled him home, and put him to work in the machine-shop. There the manager reported that, except that he had shown himself a good "mixer," and had organized picnics for the benefit societies, and a base-ball team, he had not earned his fifteen dollars a week.

When Roddy was called before him, his father said:

"It is wrong that your rare talents as a 'mixer' should be wasted in front of a turning-lathe. Callahan tells me you can talk your way through boiler-plate, so I am going to give you a chance to talk the Japs into giving us a contract. But, remember this, Roddy," his father continued sententiously, "the Japs are the Jews of the present. Be polite, but don't appear *too* anxious. If you do, they will beat you down in the price."

Perhaps this parting injunction explains why, from the time Roddy first burst upon the Land of the Rising Sun, he had devoted himself entirely to the Yokohama tea-houses and the base-ball grounds of the American Naval Hospital. He was trying, he said, not to appear too anxious. He hoped father would be pleased.

With Roddy to Japan, as a companion, friend and fellow-tourist, came Peter de Peyster, who hailed from the banks of the Hudson, and of what Roddy called "one of our ancient poltroon families." At Yale, although he had been two classes in advance of Roddy, the two had been roommates, and such firm friends that they contradicted each other without ceasing. Having quarrelled through two years of college life, they were on terms of such perfect understanding as to be inseparable.

The third youth was the "Orchid Hunter." His father manufactured the beer that, so Roddy said, had made his home town bilious. He was not really an orchid hunter, but on his journeyings around the globe he had become so ashamed of telling people he had no other business than to spend his father's money that he had decided to say he was collecting orchids.

"It shows imagination," he explained, "and I have spent enough money on orchids on Fifth Avenue to make good."

The fourth youth in the group wore the uniform and insignia of a Lieutenant of the United States Navy. His name was Perry, and, looking down from the toy balcony of the tea-house, clinging like a bird's-nest to the face of the rock, they could see his battle-ship on the berth. It was Perry who had convoyed them to O Kin San and her delectable tea-house, and it was Perry who was talking shop.

"But the most important member of the ship's company on a submarine," said the sailorman, "doesn't draw any pay at all, and he has no rating. He is a mouse."

"He's a *what?*" demanded the Orchid Hunter.

THE WHITE MICE

He had been patriotically celebrating the arrival of the American Squadron. During tiffin, the sight of the white uniforms in the hotel dining-room had increased his patriotism; and after tiffin the departure of the Pacific Mail, carrying to the Golden Gate so many "good fellows," further aroused it. Until the night before, in the billiard-room, he had never met any of the good fellows; but the thought that he might never see them again now depressed him. And the tea he was drinking neither cheered nor inebriated. So when the Orchid Hunter spoke he showed a touch of temper.

"Don't talk sea slang to me," he commanded; "when you say he is a mouse, what do you mean by a mouse?"

"I mean a mouse," said the Lieutenant, "a white mouse with pink eyes. He bunks in the engine-room, and when he smells sulphuric gas escaping anywhere he squeals; and the chief finds the leak, and the ship isn't blown up. Sometimes, one little, white mouse will save the lives of a dozen bluejackets."

Roddy and Peter de Peyster nodded appreciatively.

"Mos' extr'd'n'ry!" said the Orchid Hunter. "Mos' sad, too. I will now drink to the mouse. The moral of the story is," he pointed out, "that everybody, no matter how impecunious,

THE WHITE MICE

can help; even you fellows could help. So could I."

His voice rose in sudden excitement. "I will now," he cried, "organize the Society of the Order of the White Mice. The object of the society is to save everybody's life. Don't tell me," he objected scornfully, "that you fellows will let a little white mice save twelve hundred bluejackets, an' you sit there an' grin. You mus' all be a White Mice. You mus' all save somebody's life. An'—then—then we give ourself a dinner."

"And medals!" suggested Peter de Peyster.

The Orchid Hunter frowned. He regarded the amendment with suspicion.

"Is't th' intention of the Hon'ble Member from N'York," he asked, "that *each* of us gets a medal, or just th' one that does th' saving?"

"Just one," said Peter de Peyster.

"No, we all get 'em," protested Roddy. "Each time!"

"Th' 'men'ment to th' 'men'ment is carried," announced the Orchid Hunter. He untwisted his legs and clapped his hands. The paper walls slid apart, the little Nezans, giggling, bowing, ironing out their knees with open palms, came tripping and stumbling to obey.

"Take away the tea!" shouted the Orchid Hunter. "It makes me nervous. Bring us

THE WHITE MICE

fizzy-water, in larges' size, cold, expensive bottles. And now, you fellows," proclaimed the Orchid Hunter, "I'm goin' into secret session and initiate you into Yokohama Chapter, Secret Order of White Mice. And—I will be Mos' Exalted Secret White Mouse."

When he returned to the ship Perry told the wardroom about it and laughed, and the wardroom laughed, and that night at the Grand Hotel, while the Japanese band played "Give My Regards to Broadway," which Peter de Peyster told them was the American national anthem, the White Mice gave their first annual dinner. For, as the Orchid Hunter pointed out, in order to save life, one must sustain it.

And Louis Eppinger himself designed that dinner, and the Paymaster, and Perry's brother officers, who were honored guests, still speak of it with awe; and the next week's *Box of Curios* said of it editorially: "And while our little Yokohama police know much of ju-jitsu, they found that they had still something to learn of the short jab to the jaw and the quick getaway."

Indeed, throughout, it was a most successful dinner.

And just to show how small this world is, and that "God moves in a mysterious way, His wonders to perform," at three o'clock that morning, when the dinner-party in rickshaws were rolling down the Bund, singing "We're Little White Mice Who Have Gone Astray," their voices carried across the Pacific, across the Cordilleras and the Caribbean Sea; and an old man in his cell, tossing and shivering with fever, smiled and sank to sleep; for in his dreams he had heard the scampering feet of the White Mice, and he had seen the gates of his prison-cell roll open.

The Forrester Construction Company did not get the contract to build the three light-houses. The Japanese preferred a light-house made by an English firm. They said it was cheaper. It *was* cheaper, because they bought the working plans from a draftsman the English firm had discharged for drunkenness, and, by causing the revolving light to wink once instead of twice, dodged their own patent laws.

Mr. Forrester agreed with the English firm that the Japanese were "a wonderful little people," and then looked about for some one individual he could blame. Finding no one else, he blamed Roddy. The interview took place on the twenty-seventh story of the Forrester Building, in a room that overlooked the Brooklyn Bridge.

"You didn't fall down on the job," the fond

parent was carefully explaining, "because you never were *on* the job. You didn't even *start*. It was thoughtful of you to bring back kimonos to mother and the girls. But the one you brought me does not entirely compensate me for the ninety thousand dollars you didn't bring back. I would *like* my friends to see me in a kimono with silk storks and purple wistarias down the front, but I feel I cannot afford to pay ninety thousand dollars for a bath-robe.

"Nor do I find," continued the irate parent coldly, "that the honor you did the company by disguising yourself as a stoker and helping the base-ball team of the *Louisiana* to win the pennant of the Asiatic Squadron, altogether reconciles us to the loss of a government contract. I have paid a good deal to have you taught mechanical engineering, and I should like to know how soon you expect to give me the interest on my money."

Roddy grinned sheepishly, and said he would begin at once, by taking his father out to lunch.

"Good!" said Forrester, Senior. "But before we go, Roddy, I want you to look over there to the Brooklyn side. Do you see pier number eleven—just south of the bridge? Yes? Then do you see a white steamer taking on supplies?"

Roddy, delighted at the change of subject, nodded.

THE WHITE MICE

"That ship," continued his father, "is sailing to Venezuela, where we have a concession from the government to build breakwaters and buoy the harbors and put up light-houses. We have been working there for two years and we've spent about two million dollars. And some day we hope to get our money. Sometimes," continued Mr. Forrester, "it is necessary to throw good money after bad. That is what we are doing in Venezuela."

"I don't understand," interrupted Roddy with polite interest.

"You are not expected to," said his father. "If you will kindly condescend to hold down the jobs I give you, you can safely leave the high finance of the company to your father."

"Quite so," said Roddy hastily. "Where shall we go to lunch?"

As though he had not heard him, Forrester, Senior, continued relentlessly: "To-morrow," he said, "you are sailing on that ship for Porto Cabello; we have just started a light-house at Porto Cabello, and are buoying the harbor. You are going for the F. C. C. You are an inspector."

Roddy groaned and sank into a chair.

"Go on," he commanded, "break it to me quick! *What* do I inspect?"

"You sit in the sun," said Mr. Forrester, "with a pencil, and every time our men empty

THE WHITE MICE

a bag of cement into the ocean you make a mark. At the same time, if you are not an utter idiot and completely blind, you can't help but see how a light-house is set up. The company is having trouble in Venezuela, trouble in collecting its money. You might as well know that, because everybody in Venezuela will tell you so. But that's all you need to know. The other men working for the company down there will think, because you are my son, that you know more about what I'm doing in Venezuela than they do. Now, understand, you don't know anything, and I want you to say so. I want you to stick to your own job, and not mix up in anything that doesn't concern you. There will be nothing to distract you. McKildrick writes me that in Porto Cabello there are no tea-houses, no roads for automobiles, and, except for the fire-flies, all the white lights go out at nine o'clock.

"Now, Roddy," concluded Mr. Forrester warningly, "this is your chance, and it is the last chance for dinner in the dining-car, for you. If you fail the company, and by the company I mean myself, *this* time, you can ask Fred Sterry for a job on the waiters' nine at Palm Beach."

Like all the other great captains, Mr. Forrester succeeded through the work of his lieu-

THE WHITE MICE

tenants. For him, in every part of the world, more especially in those parts of it in which the white man was but just feeling his way, they were at work.

In Siberia, in British East Africa, in Upper Burmah, engineers of the Forrester Construction Company had tamed, shackled and bridged great rivers. In the Soudan they had thrown up ramparts against the Nile. Along the coasts of South America they had cast the rays of the Forrester revolving light upon the face of the waters of both the South Atlantic and the Pacific.

They were of all ages, from the boys who had never before looked through a transit except across the college campus, to sun-tanned, fever-haunted veterans who, for many years, had fought Nature where she was most stubborn, petulant and cruel. They had seen a tidal-wave crumple up a breakwater which had cost them a half-year of labor, and slide it into the ocean. They had seen swollen rivers, drunk with the rains, trip bridges by the ankles and toss them on the banks, twisted and sprawling; they had seen a tropical hurricane overturn a half-finished light-house as gayly as a summer breeze upsets a rocking-chair; they had fought with wild beasts, they had fought with wild men, with Soudanese of the Desert,

THE WHITE MICE

with Federated Sons of Labor, with Yaqui Indians, and they had seen cholera, sleeping-sickness and the white man's gin turn their compounds into pest-camps and crematories.

Of these things Mr. Forrester, in the twenty-seven-story Forrester sky-scraper, where gray-coated special policemen and elevator-starters touched their caps to him, had seen nothing. He regarded these misadventures by flood and field only as obstacles to his carrying out in the time stipulated a business contract. He accepted them patiently as he would a strike of the workmen on the apartment-house his firm was building on Fifty-ninth Street.

Sometimes, in order to better show the progress they were making, his engineers sent him from strange lands photographs of their work. At these, for a moment, he would glance curiously, at the pictures of naked, dark-skinned coolies in turbans, of elephants dragging iron girders, *his* iron girders; and perhaps he would wonder if the man in the muddy boots and the heavy sun hat was McKenzie. His interest went no further than that; his imagination was not stirred.

Sometimes McKenzie returned and, in evening dress, dined with him at his up-town club, or at a fashionable restaurant, where the senses of the engineer were stifled by the steam heat, the music and the scent of flowers; where, through a joyous mist of red candle-shades and golden champagne, he once more looked upon women of his own color. It was not under such conditions that Mr. Forrester could expect to know the real McKenzie. This was not the McKenzie who, two months before, was fighting death on a diet of fruit salts, and who, against the sun, wore a bath-towel down his spinal column. On such occasions Mr. Forrester wanted to know if, with native labor costing but a few yards of cotton and a bowl of rice, the new mechanical rivet-drivers were not an extravagance. How, he would ask, did salt water and a sweating temperature of one hundred and five degrees act upon the new anti-rust paint? That was what he wanted to know.

Once one of his young lieutenants, inspired by a marvellous dinner, called to him across the table: "You remember, sir, that light-house we put up in the Persian Gulf? The Consul at Aden told me, this last trip, that before that light was there the wrecks on the coast averaged fifteen a year and the deaths from drowning over a hundred. You will be glad to hear that since your light went up, three years ago, there have been only two wrecks and no deaths."

Mr. Forrester nodded gravely.

"I remember," he said. "That was the time

THE WHITE MICE

we made the mistake of sending cement through the Canal instead of around the Cape, and the tolls cost us five thousand dollars."

It was not that Mr. Forrester weighed the loss of the five thousand dollars against a credit of lives saved. It was rather that he was not in the life-saving business. Like all his brother captains, he was, in a magnificent way, mechanically charitable. For institutions that did make it a business to save life he wrote large checks. But he never mixed charity and business. In what he was doing in the world he either was unable to see, or was not interested in seeing, what was human, dramatic, picturesque. When he forced himself to rest from his labor, his relaxation was the reading of novels of romance, of adventure—novels that told of strange places and strange peoples. Between the after-dinner hour and bedtime, or while his yacht picked her way up the Sound, these tales filled him with surprise. Often he would exclaim admiringly: "I don't see how these fellows think up such things."

He did not know that, in his own business, there were melodramas, romances which made those of the fiction-writers ridiculous.

And so, when young Sam Caldwell, the third vice-president, told Mr. Forrester that if the company hoped to obtain the money it had

THE WHITE MICE

sunk in Venezuela it must finance a revolution, Mr. Forrester, without question, consented to the expense, and put it down under "Political." Had Sam Caldwell shown him that what was needed was a construction-raft or a half-dozen giant steam-shovels, he would have furnished the money as readily and with as little curiosity.

Sam Caldwell, the third vice-president, was a very smart young man. Every one, even men much older than he, said as much, and no one was more sure of it than was Sam Caldwell himself. His vanity on that point was, indeed, his most prepossessing human quality.

He was very proud of his freedom from those weak scruples that prevented rival business men from underbidding the F. C. C. He congratulated himself on the fact that at thirty-four he was much more of a cynic than men of sixty. He held no illusions, and he rejoiced in a sense of superiority over those of his own class in college, who, in matters of business, were still hampered by old-time traditions.

If in any foreign country the work of the F. C. C. was halted by politicians, it was always Sam Caldwell who was sent across the sea to confer with them. He could quote you the market-price on a Russian grand-duke, or a Portuguese colonial governor, as accurately as

THE WHITE MICE

he could that of a Tammany sachem. His was the non-publicity department. People who did not like him called him Mr. Forrester's jackal. When the lawyers of the company had studied how they could evade the law on corporations, and had shown how the officers of the F. C. C. could do a certain thing and still keep out of jail, Sam Caldwell was the man who did that thing.

He had been to Venezuela "to look over the ground," and he had reported that President Alvarez must go, and that some one who would be friendly to the F. C. C. must be put in his place. That was all Mr. Forrester knew, or cared to know. With the delay in Venezuela he was impatient. He wanted to close up that business and move his fleet of tenders, dredges and rafts to another coast. So, as was the official routine, he turned over the matter to Sam Caldwell, to settle it in Sam Caldwell's own way.

Two weeks after his talk with his father, Roddy, ignorant of Mr. Caldwell's intentions, was in Venezuela, sitting on the edge of a construction-raft, dangling his rubber boots in the ocean, and watching a steel skeleton creep up from a coral reef into a blazing, burning sky. At intervals he would wake to remove his cigarette, and shout fiercely: "*O-i-i-ga,* you

THE WHITE MICE

Moso! Get a move on! *Pronto!* If you don't I'll do that myself."

Every ten minutes El Señor Roddy had made the same threat, and the workmen, once hopeful that he would carry it into effect, had grown despondent.

In the mind of Peter de Peyster there was no doubt that, unless something was done, and at once, the Order of the White Mice would cease to exist. The call of Gain, of Duty, of Pleasure had scattered the charter members to distant corners of the world. Their dues were unpaid, the pages of the Golden Book of Record were blank. Without the necessary quorum of two there could be no meetings, without meetings there could be no dinners, and, incidentally, over all the world people continued to die, and the White Mice were doing nothing to prevent it. Peter de Peyster, mindful of his oath, of his duty as the Most Secret Secretary and High Historian of the Order, shot arrows in the air in the form of irate postal-cards. He charged all White Mice to instantly report to the Historian the names of those persons whom, up to date, they had saved from death.

From the battle-ship *Louisiana*, Perry wrote briefly:

THE WHITE MICE

"Beg to report during gale off Finisterre, went to rescue of man overboard. Man overboard proved to be Reagan, gunner's mate, first class, holding long-distance championship for swimming and two medals for saving life. After I sank the third time, Reagan got me by the hair and towed me to the ship. Who gets the assist?"

From Raffles' Hotel, Singapore, the Orchid Hunter cabled:

"Have saved own valuable life by refusing any longer to drink Father's beer. Give everybody medal."

From Porto Cabello, Venezuela, Roddy wrote:

"I have saved lives of fifty Jamaica coolies daily by not carrying an axe. If you want to save my life from suicide, sunstroke and sleeping-sickness—which attacks me with special virulence immediately after lunch—come by next steamer."

A week later, Peter de Peyster took the Red D boat south, and after touching at Porto Rico and at the Island of Curaçao, swept into Porto Cabello and into the arms of his friend.

On the wharf, after the shouts of welcome had died away, Roddy inquired anxiously: "As you made the harbor, Peter, did you notice any red and black buoys? Those are *my* buoys. I put them there—*myself*. And I laid out that

THE WHITE MICE

entire channel you came in by, all by myself, too!"

Much time had passed since the two friends had been able to insult each other face to face.

"Roddy," coldly declared Peter, "if I thought *you* had charted that channel I'd go home on foot, by land."

"Do you mean you think I can't plant deep-sea buoys?" demanded Roddy.

"You can't plant potatoes!" said Peter. "If you had to set up lamp-posts, with the street names on them, along Broadway, you would put the ones marked Union Square in Columbus Circle."

"I want you to know," shouted Roddy, "that my buoys are the talk of this port. These people are just crazy about my buoys—especially the red buoys. If you didn't come to Venezuela to see my buoys, why did you come? I will plant a buoy for you to-morrow!" challenged Roddy. "I will show you!"

"You will *have* to show me," said Peter.

Peter had been a week in Porto Cabello, and, in keeping Roddy at work, had immensely enjoyed himself. Each morning, in the company's gasolene launch, the two friends went put-put-putting outside the harbor, where Roddy made soundings for his buoys, and Peter lolled in the stern and fished. His special pleasure was in trying to haul man-eating sharks into the launch at the moment Roddy was leaning over the gunwale, taking a sounding.

One evening at sunset, on their return trip, as they were under the shadow of the fortress, the engine of the launch broke down. While the black man from Trinidad was diagnosing the trouble, Peter was endeavoring to interest Roddy in the quaint little Dutch Island of Curaçao that lay one hundred miles to the east of them. He chose to talk of Curaçao because the ship that carried him from the States had touched there, while the ship that brought Roddy south had not. This fact irritated Roddy, so Peter naturally selected the moment when the launch had broken down and Roddy was both hungry and peevish to talk of Curaçao.

"Think of your never having seen Curaçao!" he sighed. "Some day you certainly must visit it. With a sea as flat as this is to-night you could make the run in the launch in twelve hours. It is a place you should see."

"That is *so* like you," exclaimed Roddy indignantly. "I have been here four months, and you have been here a week, and you try to tell *me* about Curaçao! It is the place where curaçao and revolutionists come from. All the exiles from Venezuela wait over there until there

THE WHITE MICE

is a revolution over here, and then they come across. You can't tell *me* anything about Curaçao. *I* don't have to *go* to a place to know about it."

"I'll bet," challenged Peter, "you don't know about the mother and the two daughters who were exiled from Venezuela and live in Curaçao, and who look over here every night at sunset?"

Roddy laughed scornfully. "Why, that is the first thing they tell you," he cried; "the purser points them out from the ship, and tells you——"

"Tells *you*, yes," cried Peter triumphantly, "but I *saw* them. As we left the harbor they were standing on the cliff—three women in white—looking toward Venezuela. They told me the father of the two girls is in prison here. He was——"

"*Told* you, yes," mimicked Roddy, "told you he was in prison. I have *seen* him in prison. There is the prison."

Roddy pointed at the flat, yellow fortress that rose above them. Behind the tiny promontory on which the fortress crouched was the town, separated from it by a stretch of water so narrow that a golf-player, using the quay of the custom-house for a tee, could have driven a ball against the prison wall.

THE WHITE MICE

Daily, from the town, Peter had looked across the narrow harbor toward the level stretch of limestone rock that led to the prison gates, and had seen the petty criminals, in chains, splash through the pools left by the falling tide, had watched each pick up a cask of fresh water, and, guarded by the barefooted, red-capped soldiers, drag his chains back to the prison. Now, only the boat's-length from them, he saw the sheer face of the fortress, where it slipped to depths unknown into the sea. It impressed him most unpleasantly. It had the look less of a fortress than of a neglected tomb. Its front was broken by wind and waves, its surface, blotched and mildewed, white with crusted salt, hideous with an eruption of dead barnacles. As each wave lifted and retreated, leaving the porous wall dripping like a sponge, it disturbed countless crabs, rock scorpions and creeping, leech-like things that ran blindly into the holes in the limestone; and, at the water-line, the sea-weed, licking hungrily at the wall, rose and fell, the great arms twisting and coiling like the tentacles of many devil-fish.

Distaste at what he saw, or the fever that at sunset drives wise Venezuelans behind closed shutters, caused Peter to shiver slightly.

For some moments, with grave faces and in silence, the two young men sat motionless, the mind of each trying to conceive what life must be behind those rusted bars and moss-grown walls.

"Somewhere, buried in there," said Roddy, "is General Rojas, the Lion of Valencia, a man," he added sententiously, "beloved by the people. He has held all the cabinet positions, and been ambassador in Europe, and Alvarez is more afraid of him than of any other man in Venezuela. And why? For the simple reason that he is good. When the people found out what a blackguard Alvarez is they begged Rojas to run for President against him, and Rojas promised that if, at the next election, the people still desired it, he would do as they wished. That night Alvarez hauled him out of bed and put him in there. He has been there two years. There *are* healthy prisons, but Alvarez put Rojas in this one, hoping it would kill him. He is afraid to murder him openly, because the people love him. When I first came here I went through the fortress with Vicenti, the prison doctor, on a sort of Seeing-Porto-Cabello trip. He pointed out Rojas to me through the bars, same as you would point out a monument to a dead man. Rojas was sitting at a table, writing, wrapped in a shawl. The cell was lit by a candle, and I give you my word, although it was blazing hot outside, the place was as

THE WHITE MICE

damp as a refrigerator. When we raised our lanterns he stood up, and I got a good look at him. He is a thin, frail little man with white hair and big, sad eyes, with a terribly lonely look in them. At least I thought so; and I felt so ashamed at staring at him that I bowed and salamed to him through the bars, and he gave me the most splendid bow, just as though he were still an ambassador and I a visiting prince. The doctor had studied medicine in New York, so probably he talked to me a little more freely than he should. He says he warned the commandant of the fortress that unless Rojas is moved to the upper tier of cells, above the water-line, he will die in six months. And the commandant told him not to meddle in affairs of state, that his orders from the President were that Rojas 'must never again feel the heat of the sun.'"

Peter de Peyster exclaimed profanely. "Are there no men in this country?" he growled. "Why don't his friends get him out?"

"They'd have to get themselves out first," explained Roddy. "Alvarez made a clean sweep of it, even of his wife and his two daughters, the women you saw. He exiled them, and they went to Curaçao. They have plenty of money, and they *could* have lived in Paris or London. He has been minister in both places,

27

THE WHITE MICE

and has many friends over there, but even though they cannot see him or communicate with him, they settled down in Curaçao so that they might be near him.

"The night his wife was ordered out of the country she was allowed to say good-by to him in the fortress, and there she arranged that every night at sunset she and her daughters would look toward Porto Cabello, and he would look toward Curaçao. The women bought a villa on the cliff, to the left of the harbor of Willemstad as you enter, and the people, the Dutch and the Spaniards and negroes, all know the story, and when they see the three women on the cliff at sunset it is like the Angelus ringing, and, they say, the people pray that the women may see him again."

For a long time Peter de Peyster sat scowling at the prison, and Roddy did not speak, for it is not possible to room with another man through two years of college life and not know something of his moods.

Then Peter leaned toward Roddy and stared into his face. His voice carried the suggestion of a challenge.

"I hear something!" he whispered.

Whether his friend spoke in metaphor or stated a fact, Roddy could not determine. He looked at him questioningly, and raised his head to listen. Save for the whisper of the waves against the base of the fortress, there was no sound.

"What?" asked Roddy.

"I hear the call of the White Mice," said Peter de Peyster.

There was a long silence. Then Roddy laughed softly, his eyes half closed; the muscles around the lower jaw drew tight.

Often before Peter had seen the look in his face, notably on a memorable afternoon when Roddy went to the bat, with three men on base, two runs needed to win the championship and twenty thousand shrieking people trying to break his nerve.

"I will go as far as you like," said Roddy.

Porto Cabello is laid out within the four boundaries of a square. The boundary on the east and the boundary on the north of the square meet at a point that juts into the harbor. The wharves and the custom-house, looking toward the promontory on which stands the fortress prison, form the eastern side of the square, and along the northern edge are the Aquatic Club, with its veranda over the water, the hotel, with its bath-rooms underneath the water, and farther along the harbor front houses set in gardens. As his work was in the harbor,

Roddy had rented one of these houses. It was discreetly hidden by mango-trees and palmetto, and in the rear of the garden, steps cut in the living rock led down into the water. In a semi-circle beyond these steps was a fence of bamboo stout enough to protect a bather from the harbor sharks and to serve as a breakwater for the launch.

"When I rented this house," said Roddy, "I thought I took it because I could eat mangoes while I was in bathing and up to my ears in water, which is the only way you can eat a mango and keep your self-respect. But I see now that Providence sent me here because we can steal away in the launch without any one knowing it."

"If you can move that launch its own length without the whole town knowing it," commented Peter, "you will have to chloroform it. It barks like a machine gun."

"My idea was," explained Roddy, "that we would row to the fortress. After we get the General on board, the more it sounds like a machine gun the better."

Since their return in the launch, and during dinner, which had been served in the tiny *patio* under the stars, the White Mice had been discussing ways and means. A hundred plans had been proposed, criticised, rejected; but by one in the morning, when the candles were guttering in the harbor breeze and the Scotch whiskey had shrunk several inches, the conspirators found themselves agreed. They had decided they could do nothing until they knew in which cell the General was imprisoned, and especially the position of his window in that cell that looked out upon the harbor; that, with the aid of the launch, the rescue must be made from the water, and that the rescuers must work from the outside. To get at Rojas from the inside it would be necessary to take into their confidence some one of the prison officials, and there was no one they dared to trust. Had it been a question of money, Roddy pointed out, the friends of Rojas would already have set him free. That they had failed to do so proved, not that the prison officials were incorruptible, but that their fear of the wrath of Alvarez was greater than their cupidity.

"There are several reasons why we should not attempt to bribe any one," said Roddy, "and the best one is the same reason the man gave for not playing poker. To-morrow I will introduce you to Vicenti, the prison doctor, and we'll ask him to take us over the prison, and count the cells, and try to mark the one in which we see Rojas. Perhaps we'd better have the doctor in to dinner. He likes to tell you what a devil of a fellow he was in New York, and you must pretend to believe he was. We might also have the captain of the port, and get him to give us permission to take the launch out at night. This port is still under martial law, and after the sunset gun no boat may move about the harbor. Then we must have some harpoons made and get out that headlight, and spear eels."

"You couldn't spear an eel," objected Peter, "and if you could I wouldn't eat it."

"You don't have to eat it!" explained Roddy; "the eels are only an excuse. We want to get the sentries used to seeing us flashing around the harbor at night. If we went out there without some excuse, and without permission, exploding like a barrel of fire-crackers, they'd sink us. So we must say we are out spearing eels."

The next morning Roddy showed a blacksmith how to hammer out tridents for spearing eels, and that night those people who lived along the harbor front were kept awake by quick-fire explosions, and the glare in their windows of a shifting search-light. But at the end of the week the launch of the Gringos, as it darted noisily in and out of the harbor, and carelessly flashed its search-light on the walls of the fortress, came to be regarded less as a nuisance than a blessing. For with noble self-sacrifice the harbor eels lent themselves to the deception. By hundreds they swarmed in front of the dazzling headlight; by dozens they impaled themselves upon the tines of the pitchforks. So expert did Roddy and Peter become in harpooning, that soon they were able each morning to send to the captain of the port, to the commandant, to the prison doctor, to every citizen who objected to having his sleep punctuated, a basket of eels. It was noticed that at intervals the engine of the launch would not act properly, and the Gringos were seen propelling the boat with oars. Also, the light often went out, leaving them in darkness. They spoke freely of these accidents with bitter annoyance, and people sympathized with them.

One night, when they were seated plotting in the *patio*, Roddy was overwhelemd with sudden misgivings.

"Wouldn't it be awful," he cried, "if, after we have cut the bars and shown him the rope ladder and the launch, he refuses to come with us!"

"Is that *all* that's worrying you?" asked Peter.

"How is he to know?" persisted Roddy, "that we are not paid by Alvarez, that we aren't leading him on to escape so that the sentries can have an excuse to shoot him. That has been done before. It is an old trick, like killing a man in his cell and giving out that he committed suicide. The first thing Rojas will ask us is, who sends us, and where are our credentials."

"I guess he will take his chance," said Peter. "He'll see we are not Venezuelans."

"That is the very thing that will make him refuse," protested Roddy. "Why should he trust himself to strangers—to Gringos? No, I tell you, we can't go on without credentials." He lowered his voice and glanced suspiciously into the dark corners of the *patio*. "And the only people who can give them to us," he added, tapping impressively upon the table, "live in Curaçao."

With sudden enthusiasm Peter de Peyster sat upright.

"I am on in that scene," he protested.

"I thought of it first," said Roddy.

"We will toss," compromised Peter. "The head of Bolivar, you go. The arms of Venezuela, I go, and you stay here and catch eels."

The silver peso rang upon the table, and Roddy exclaimed jubilantly:

"Heads! I go!" he cried. But the effort of Peter to show he was not disappointed was so unconvincing that Roddy instantly relented.

THE WHITE MICE

"We had better both go!" he amended. "Your headwork is better than mine, so you come, too. And if you give me the right signals, I'll try to put the ball where you can reach it."

As though in his eagerness he would set forth on the instant, Roddy sprang to his feet and stood smiling down at Peter, his face lit with pleasurable excitement. Then suddenly his expression grew thoughtful.

"Peter," he inquired, "how old do you think the daughters are?"

II

THE next day Roddy and Peter sailed for Willemstad, the chief port and the capital of the tiny island colony of Holland. In twelve hours they had made their land-fall and were entering the harbor mouth. The sun was just rising, and as its rays touched the cliff from which, twelve hours later, Señora Rojas and her daughters would look toward Porto Cabello, they felt a thrill of possible adventure.

Roddy knew that, as a refuge for revolutionists exiled from Venezuela, Willemstad was policed with secret agents of Alvarez, and he knew that were these spies to learn that during his visit either he or Peter had called upon the family of Rojas they would be reported to Caracas as "suspect," and the chance of their saving the Lion of Valencia would be at an end. So it became them to be careful.

Before leaving Porto Cabello Roddy had told McKildrick, the foreman of the Construction Company's work there, that some boxes of new machinery and supplies for his launch had gone astray and that he wished permission to cross to Curaçao to look them up. McKildrick believed the missing boxes were only an excuse for a holiday, but he was not anxious to assert his authority over the son and heir of the F. C. C., and so gave Roddy his leave of absence. And at the wharf at Porto Cabello, while waiting for the ship to weigh anchor, Roddy had complained to the custom-house officials at having to cross to Curaçao. He gave them the same reason for the trip, and said it was most annoying.

In order to be consistent, when, on landing at Willemstad, three soiled individuals approached Roddy and introduced themselves as guides, he told them the same story. He was looking for boxes of machinery invoiced for Porto Cabello; he feared they had been carried on to La Guayra or dropped at Willemstad. Could they direct him to the office of the steamship line and to the American Consul? One of the soiled persons led him across the quay to the office of the agent, and while Roddy repeated his complaint, listened so eagerly that to both Peter and Roddy it was quite evident the business of the guide was not to disclose Curaçao to strangers, but to learn what brought strangers to Curaçao. The agent was only too delighted to serve the son of one who in money meant so much to the line. For an hour he searched his books, his warehouse and the quays. But, naturally, the search was unsuccessful, and with most genuine apologies Roddy left him, saying that at the office of the American Consul he would continue his search for the lost boxes.

Meanwhile, Peter, in his character of tourist, engaged rooms for them at the Hotel Commercial, and started off alone to explore the town.

At the Consulate, the soiled person listened to the beginning of Roddy's speech, and then, apparently satisfied he had learned all that was necessary, retreated to the outer office.

The Consul promptly rose and closed the door.

The representative of the United States was an elderly man, of unusual height, with searching, honest blue eyes under white eyebrows. His hair was white, his beard, worn long, was white, and his clothes were of white duck.

His name was Sylvanus Cobb Codman, with the added title of captain, which he had earned when, as a younger man, he had been owner and master of one of the finest whalers that ever cleared the harbor of New Bedford. During his cruises he had found the life of the West Indies much to his liking, and when, at the age of fifty, he ceased to follow the sea, he had asked for an appointment as consul to Porto Cabello. Since then, except when at home on leave at Fairhaven, he had lived in the Spanish Americas, and at many ports had served the State Department faithfully and well. In spite of his age, Captain Codman gave a pleasant impression of strength and nervous energy. Roddy felt that the mind and body of the man were as clean as his clothes, and that the Consul was one who could be trusted.

As Captain Codman seated himself behind his desk he was frowning.

"You must look out for that guide," he said. "He is from Caracas. He is an agent of Alvarez. It just shows," he went on impatiently, "what little sense these spies have, that he didn't recognize your name. The Forrester Construction Company is certainly well enough known. That the son of your father should be spied on is ridiculous."

"Then, again," said Roddy mysteriously, "maybe it isn't. I haven't got such a clean bill of health. That's why I came to you." With an air which he considered was becoming in a conspirator, he lowered his voice. "May I ask, sir," he said, "if you are acquainted with Señora Rojas, who is in exile here?"

The blue eyes of the Consul opened slightly, but he answered with directness, "I am. I have that honor."

THE WHITE MICE

"And with her daughters?" added Roddy anxiously.

With dignity the Consul inclined his head.

"I want very much to meet them—her," corrected Roddy. "I am going to set her husband free!"

For a moment, as though considering whether he were not confronted by a madman, the Consul regarded Roddy with an expression of concern. Then, in the deprecatory tone of one who believes he has not heard aright, he asked, "You are going to do—*what?*"

"I am going to help General Rojas to escape," Roddy went on briskly—"myself and another fellow. But we are afraid he won't trust himself to us, so I am over here to get credentials from his wife. But, you see, I have first got to get credentials to her. So I came to ask you if you'd sort of vouch for me, tell her who I am—and all that."

The Consul was staring at him so strangely that Roddy believed he had not made himself fully understood.

"You know what I mean," he explained. "Credentials, something he will know came from her—a ring or a piece of paper saying, 'These are friends. Go with them.' Or a lock of her hair, or—or—you know," urged Roddy in embarrassment—"credentials."

"Are you jesting?" asked the older man coldly.

Roddy felt genuinely uncomfortable. He was conscious he was blushing. "Certainly not," he protested. "It is serious enough, isn't it?"

The voice of the Consul dropped to a whisper. "Who sent you here?" he demanded. Without waiting for an answer he suddenly rose. Moving with surprising lightness to the door, he jerked it open. But if by this manœuvre he expected to precipitate the spy into the room, he was disappointed, for the outer office was empty. The Consul crossed it quickly to the window. He saw the spy disappearing into a neighboring wine-shop.

When Captain Codman again entered the inner office he did not return to his seat, but, after closing the door, as though to shut Roddy from the only means of escape, he stood with his back against it. He was very much excited.

"Mr. Forrester," he began angrily, "I don't know who is back of you, and," he cried violently, "I don't *mean* to know. I have been American Consul in these Central American countries for fifteen years, and I have never mixed myself up with what doesn't concern me. I represent the United States government. I don't represent anything else. I am not down here to assist any corporation, no matter how rich, any junta, any revolutionary party——"

"Here! Wait!" cried Roddy anxiously. "You don't understand! I am not a revolution. There is only me and Peter."

"What is that?" snapped the Consul savagely. The exclamation was like the crack of a flapping jib.

"You see, it's this way," began Roddy. He started to explain elaborately. "Peter and I belong to the Secret Order——"

"Stop!" thundered the Consul. "I tell you I won't listen to you!"

The rebuff was most embarrassing. Ignorant as to how he had offended the Consul, and uncertain as to whether the Consul had not offended him, Roddy helplessly rubbed his handkerchief over his perplexed and perspiring countenance. He wondered if, as a conspirator, he had not been lacking in finesse, if he had not been too communicative.

In the corner of the room, in a tin cage, a great green parrot, with its head cocked on one side, had been regarding Roddy with mocking, malevolent eyes. Now, to further add to his discomfiture, it suddenly emitted a chuckle, human and contemptuous. As though choking with hidden laughter, the bird gurgled feebly, "Polly, Polly." And then, in a tone of stern

THE WHITE MICE

disapproval, added briskly, "You talk too much!" At this flank attack Roddy flushed indignantly. He began to wish he had brought Peter with him, to give him the proper signals.

With his hands clinched behind him, and tossing his white beard from side to side, the Consul paced the room.

"So that is it!" he muttered. "*That* is why he left Paris. That explains the *Restaurador*. Of course," he added indignantly as he passed Roddy, throwing the words at him over his shoulder, "*that* is where the money came from!"

Roddy, now thoroughly exasperated, protested warmly: "Look here," he cried, "if you aren't careful you'll tell me something you don't want me to know."

The Consul came to an instant pause. From his great height he stood staring at his visitor, the placid depths of his blue eyes glowering with doubt and excitement.

"I give you my word," continued Roddy sulkily, "I don't know what you are talking about."

"Do you mean to tell me," demanded the old man truculently, "that you are *not* Mr. Forrester's son?"

"Certainly I am his son," cried Roddy.

"Then," returned the Consul, "perhaps you

will deny he is suing Alvarez for two million dollars gold, you will deny that he might get it if Alvarez were thrown out, you will deny that a—a certain person might ratify the concession, and pay your father for the harbor improvements he has already made? You see!" exclaimed the Consul triumphantly. "And these missing boxes!" he cried as though following up an advantage, "shall I tell you what is in them?" He lowered his voice. "Cartridges and rifles! Do you deny it?"

Roddy found that at last he was on firm ground.

"Of course I deny it," he answered, "because there are no boxes. They're only an invention of mine to get me to Curaçao. Now, you let *me* talk."

The Consul retreated behind his desk, and as Roddy spoke regarded him sternly and with open suspicion. In concluding his story Roddy said: "We have no other object in saving General Rojas than that he's an old man, that he's dying, and that Peter and I can't sleep of nights for thinking of him lying in a damp cell, not three hundred yards from us, coughing himself to death."

At the words the eyes of the Consul closed quickly; he pressed his great, tanned, freckled fingers nervously against his lip. But instantly

THE WHITE MICE

the stern look of the cross-examiner returned. "Go on," he commanded.

"If we have cut in on some one's private wire," continued Roddy, "it's an accident; and when you talk about father recovering two million dollars you are telling me things I don't know. Father is not a chatty person. He has often said to me that the only safe time to talk of what you are doing, or are going to do, is when you have done it. So, if the Venezuelan government owes the Forrester Construction Company two millions and father's making a fight for it, I am probably the last person in the world he would talk to about it. All I know is that he pays me twenty dollars a week to plant buoys. But out of working hours I can do as I please, and my friend and I please to get General Rojas out of prison." Roddy rose, smiling pleasantly. "So, if you won't introduce me to Señora Rojas," he concluded, "I guess I will have to introduce myself."

With an angry gesture the Consul motioned him to be seated. From his manner it was evident that Captain Codman was uncertain whether Roddy was or was not to be believed, that, in his perplexity, he was fearful of saying too much or too little.

"Either," the old man exclaimed angrily, "you are a very clever young man, or you are extremely ignorant. Either," he went on with increasing indignation, "they have sent you here to test me, or you know nothing, and you are blundering in where other men are doing work. If you know nothing you are going to upset the plans of those men. In any case I will have nothing further to do with you. I wash my hands of you. Good-morning."

Then, as though excusing himself, he added sharply, "Besides, you talk too much."

Roddy, deeply hurt, answered with equal asperity:

"That is what your parrot thinks. Maybe you are both wrong."

When Roddy had reached the top of the stairs leading to the street, and was on the point of disappearing, the Consul called sharply to him and followed into the hall.

"Before you go," the old man whispered earnestly, "I want you clearly to understand my position toward the Rojas family. When I was Consul in Porto Cabello, General Rojas became the best friend I had. Since I have been stationed here it has been my privilege to be of service to his wife. His daughters treat me as kindly as though I were their own grandfather. No man on earth could wish General Rojas free as much as I wish it." The voice of Captain Codman trembled. For an

THE WHITE MICE

instant his face, as though swept with sudden pain, twisted in strange lines. "No one," he protested, "could wish to serve him as I do, but I warn you if you go on with this you will land in prison yourself, and you will bring General Rojas to his death. Take my advice —and go back to Porto Cabello, and keep out of politics. Or, what is better—go home. You are too young to understand the Venezuelans, and, if you stay here, you are going to make trouble for many people. For your father, and for—for many people."

As though with the hope of finally dissuading Roddy, he added ominously, "And these Venezuelans have a nasty trick of sticking a knife——"

"Oh, you go to the devil!" retorted Roddy.

As he ran down the dark stairs and out into the glaring street he heard faintly the voice of the parrot pursuing him, with mocking and triumphant jeers.

The Consul returned slowly to his office, and, sinking into his chair, buried his face in his great, knotty hands and bent his head upon the table. A ray of sunshine, filtering through the heavy Venetian blinds, touched the white hair and turned it into silver.

For a short space, save for the scratching of the parrot at the tin bars of his cage, and the

THE WHITE MICE

steady drip, drip of the water-jar, there was no sound; then the voice of the sea-captain, as many times before it had been raised in thanksgiving in the meeting-house in Fairhaven, and from the deck of his ship as she drifted under the Southern Cross, was lifted in entreaty. The blue eyes, as the old man raised them, were wet; his bronzed fists fiercely interlocked.

"Oh, Thou," he prayed, "who walked beside me on the waters, make clear to me what I am to do. I am old, but I pray Thee to let me live to see Thine enemies perish, to see those who love Thee reunited once more, happy, at home. If, in Thy wisdom, even as Thou sent forth David against Goliath, Thou hast sent this child against Thine enemies, make that clear to me. His speech is foolish, but his heart seems filled with pity. What he would do, I would do. But the way is very dark. If I serve this boy, may I serve Thee? Teach me!"

Outside the Consulate, Roddy found his convoy, the guide, waiting for him, and, to allay the suspicion of that person, gave him a cable to put on the wire for McKildrick. It read: "No trace of freight; it may come next steamer; will wait."

He returned to the agent of the line and told him he now believed the freight had been left behind in New York and that he would

THE WHITE MICE

remain in Willemstad until the arrival of the next steamer, which was due in three days.

At the hotel he found Peter anxiously awaiting him. Having locked themselves in the room the two conspirators sat down to talk things over. From what had escaped the Consul, Roddy pointed out certain facts that seemed evident: Alvarez had not paid the Forrester Construction Company, or, in a word, his father, for the work already completed in the last two years. His father, in order to obtain his money, was interested in some scheme to get rid of Alvarez and in his place put some one who would abide by the terms of the original concession. This some one might be Rojas, and then, again, might not. As Peter suggested, the Construction Company might prefer to back a candidate for president, who, while he might not be so welcome to the Venezuelans, would be more amenable to the wishes of the F. C. C. It also would probably prefer to assist a man younger than Rojas, one more easily controlled, perhaps one less scrupulously honest. It also seemed likely that if, by revolution, the men of the Construction Company intended to put in the field a candidate of their own, they would choose one with whom they could consult daily, not one who, while he might once have been a popular idol, had for the last two years been buried from the sight of man, and with whom it now was impossible to communicate.

The longer they discussed the matter the more sure they became that Rojas could not be the man for whom the Construction Company was plotting.

"If Rojas isn't the choice of the F. C. C.," argued Roddy, "his being free, or in prison, does not interest them in the least. While, on the other hand, if Rojas *is* the candidate father is backing, the sooner he is out of prison the better for everybody."

"Anyway," added Roddy, with the airy fatalism of one who nails his banner to the mast, "if my father is going to lose two millions because you and I set an old man free, then father is going to lose two millions."

Having arrived at this dutiful conclusion Roddy proposed that, covertly, in the guise of innocent sight-seers, they should explore the town, and from a distance reconnoitre the home of Señora Rojas. They accordingly hired one of the public landaus of Willemstad and told the driver to show them the places of interest.

But in Willemstad there are no particular places of interest. It is the place itself that

THE WHITE MICE

is of interest. It is not like any other port in the world.

"It used to be," Roddy pointed out, "that every comic opera had one act on a tropical island. Then some fellow discovered Holland, and now all comic operas run to blonde girls in patched breeches and wooden shoes, and the back drops are 'Rotterdam, Amsterdam, any damn place at all.' But this town combines both the ancient and modern schools. Its scene is from Miss Hook of Holland, and the girls are out of Bandanna Land."

Willemstad is compact and tiny, with a miniature governor and palace. It is painted with all the primary colors, and, though rain seldom falls on Curaçao Island, it is as clean as though the minute before it had been washed by a spring shower and put out in the sun to dry. Saint Ann Bay, which is the harbor of Willemstad, is less of a bay than a canal. On entering it a captain from his bridge can almost see what the people in the houses on either bank are eating for breakfast. These houses are modelled like those that border the canals of The Hague. They have the same peaked roofs, the front running in steps to a point, the flat façades, the many stories. But they are painted in the colors of tropical Spanish-America, in pink, yellow, cobalt blue, and behind the peaked points are scarlet tiles. Under the southern sun they are so brilliant, so theatrical, so unreal, that they look like the houses of a Noah's Ark fresh from the toy shop. There are two towns: Willemstad, and, joined to it by bridges, Otrabanda. It is on the Willemstad side that the ships tie up, and where, from the deck to the steamer, one can converse quite easily with the Monsanto brothers in their drawing-room, or with the political exiles on the balconies of the Hotel Commercial. The streets are narrow and, like the streets of Holland, paved with round cobblestones as clean as a pan of rolls just ready for the oven. Willemstad is the cleanest port in the West Indies. It is the Spotless Town of the tropics. Beyond the town are the orange plantations, and the favorite drive is from Willemstad through these orange trees around the inner harbor, or the Schottegat, to Otrabanda, and so back across the drawbridge of Good Queen Emma into Willemstad. It is a drive of little over two hours, and Roddy and Peter found it altogether charming.

About three miles outside of Willemstad they came upon the former home of a rich Spanish planter, which had been turned into a restaurant, and which, once the Groot du Crot, was now the Café Ducrot. There is little shade on the Island of Curaçao and the young men dived into the shadows of the Ducrot garden as into a cool bath. Through orange trees and spreading palmettos, flowering bushes and a tangle of vines, they followed paths of pebbles, and wandered in a maze in which they lost themselves.

"It is the enchanted garden of the sleeping princess," said Peter. "And there are her sleeping attendants," he added, pointing at two waiters who were slumbering peacefully, their arms stretched out upon the marble-top tables.

It seemed heartless to awaken them, and the young men explored further until they found a stately, rambling mansion where a theatrical landlord with much rubbing of his hands brought them glasses and wonderful Holland gin.

"We must remember the Café Ducrot," said Roddy, as they drove on. "It is so quiet and peaceful."

Afterward they recalled his having said this, and the fact caused them much amusement.

From the Café Ducrot the road ran between high bushes and stunted trees that shaded it in on either side; but could not shade it completely. Then it turned toward Otrabanda along the cliff that overlooks the sea.

THE WHITE MICE

On the land side was a wall of dusky mesquite bushes, bound together by tangled vines, with here and there bending above them a wind-tortured cocoanut palm. On the east side of the road, at great distances apart, were villas surrounded by groves of such hardy trees and plants as could survive the sweep of the sea winds. "If we ask the driver," whispered Roddy, "who lives in each house, he won't suspect we are looking for any one house in particular." Accordingly, as they drew up even with a villa they rivalled each other in exclaiming over its beauty. And the driver, his local pride becoming more and more gratified, gave them the name of the owner of the house and his history.

As he approached a villa all of white stucco, with high, white pillars rising to the flat roof of the tropics, he needed no prompting, but, with the air of one sure of his effect, pulled his horses to a halt and pointed with his whip.

"That house, gentle-mans," he said, "belongs to Señora Rojas." Though the house was one hundred yards from the road, as though fearful of being overheard, the negro spoke in an impressive whisper. "She is the lady of General Rojas. He is a great General, gentle-mans, and now he be put in prison. President Alvarez, he put that General Rojas in prison, down in the water, an' he chain him to the rock, an' he put that lady in exile. President Alvarez he be very bad man.

"Every day at six o'clock that lady and the young ladies they stand on that cliff and pray for that General Rojas. You like me to drive you, gentle-mans, out here at six o'clock," he inquired insinuatingly, "an' see those ladies pray?"

"Certainly not!" exclaimed Roddy indignantly.

But Peter, more discreet, yawned and stirred impatiently. "I am just dying for something to eat!" he protested. "Let her out, driver."

For appearance's sake they drove nearly to the outskirts of Otrabanda, and then, as though perversely, Roddy declared he wanted to drive back the way they had come and breakfast at the Café Ducrot.

"Why should we eat in a hot, smelly dining-room," he demanded in tones intended to reach the driver, "when we can eat under orange trees?"

Peter, with apparent reluctance, assented.

"Oh, have it your own way," he said. "Personally, I could eat under any tree—under a gallows-tree."

For the second time they passed the Casa Blanca, and, while apparently intent on planning an extensive breakfast, their eyes photographed its every feature. Now, as the driver was not observing them, they were able to note the position of the entrances, of the windows, rising behind iron bars, from a terrace of white and black marble. They noted the wing, used as a stable for horses and carriages, and, what was of greater interest, that a hand-rail disappeared over the edge of the cliff and suggested a landing-pier below.

But of those who lived in the white palace there was no sign. It hurt Roddy to think that if, from the house, the inmates noted the two young men in a public carriage, peering at their home, they would regard the strangers only as impertinent sighters. They could not know that the eyes of the tourists were filled with pity, that, at the sight of the villa on the cliff the heart of each had quickened with kindly emotions, with excitement, with the hope of possible adventure.

Roddy clutched Peter by the wrist; with the other hand he pointed quickly. Through a narrow opening in a thicket that stood a few rods from the house Peter descried the formal lines of a tennis court. Roddy raised his eyebrows significantly. His smile was radiant, triumphant.

"Which seems to prove," he remarked enigmatically, "that certain parties of the first part are neither aged nor infirm."

His deduction gave him such satisfaction that when they drew up at the Café Ducrot he was still smiling.

Within the short hour that had elapsed since they had last seen the Ducrot garden a surprising transformation had taken place. No longer the orange grove lay slumbering in silence. No longer the waiters dozed beside the marble-topped tables. Drawn up outside the iron fence that protected the garden from the road a half-dozen fiery Venezuelan ponies under heavy saddles, and as many more fastened to landaus and dog-carts, were neighing, squealing, jangling their silver harness, and stamping holes in the highway. On the inside, through the heavy foliage of the orange trees, came the voice of the maître d'hôtel, from the kitchen the fat chef bellowed commands. The pebbles on the walks grated harshly beneath the flying feet of the waiters.

Seated at breakfast around a long table in the far end of the garden were over twenty men, and that it was in their service the restaurant had roused itself was fairly evident. The gentlemen who made up the breakfast-party were not the broadly-built, blond Dutchmen of the island, but Venezuelans. And a young and handsome Venezuelan, seated at the head of the table, and facing the entrance to the garden, was apparently the person in whose honor they were assembled. So much younger, at least in looks, than the others, was the chief guest, that Peter, who was displeased by this invasion of their sleeping palace, suggested it was a coming-of-age party.

It was some time before the signals of the Americans were regarded. Although they had established themselves at a table surrounded by flowering shrubs, and yet strategically situated not too far distant from the kitchen or the café, no one found time to wait upon them, and they finally obtained the services of one of the waiters only by the expedient of holding tightly to his flying apron. Roddy commanded him to bring whatever was being served at the large table.

"That cook," Roddy pointed out, "is too excited to bother with our order; but, if there's enough for twenty, there will be enough for two more."

Although they were scorned by the waiters, the young men were surprised to find that to the gentlemen of the birthday-party their coming was of the utmost interest, and, though the tables were much too far apart for Roddy to hear what was said, he could see that many glances were cast in his direction, that the

THE WHITE MICE

others were talking of him, and that, for some reason, his presence was most disconcerting.

Finally, under pretence of giving an order to his coachman, one of the birthday-party, both in going and returning from the gate, walked close to their table and observed them narrowly. As he all but paused in the gravel walk opposite them, Roddy said with conviction:

"No! Walter Pater never gave the Stoic philosophy a just interpretation, while to Euphuism——"

"On the contrary," interrupted Peter warmly, "Oscar Hammerstein is the ONLY impressario who can keep the pennant flying over grand opera and a roof garden. Believe me——"

With a bewildered countenance the Venezuelan hastily passed on. Placidly the two young men continued with their breakfast.

"Even if he *does* understand English," continued Roddy, "that should keep him guessing for a while."

As they, themselves, had no interest in the birthday-party, and as they had eaten nothing since early coffee on the steamer, the young men were soon deep in the joy of feasting. But they were not long to remain in peace.

From the bushes behind them there emerged suddenly and quietly a young negro. He was intelligent looking and of good appearance.

THE WHITE MICE

His white duck was freshly ironed, his straw hat sported a gay ribbon. Without for an instant hesitating between the two men, he laid a letter in front of Roddy. "For Mr. Forrester," he said, and turning, parted the bushes and, as quickly as he had come, departed.

Roddy stared at the hedge through which the messenger had vanished, and his wondering eyes turned toward the birthday-party. He found that every one at that table was regarding him intently. It was evident all had witnessed the incident. Roddy wondered if it were possible that the letter came from them. Looking further he observed that the man who was serving Peter and himself also was regarding him wth greater interest than seemed natural, and that he was not the man who first had waited upon them.

"You," began Roddy doubtfully, "you are not the waiter who——"

The man shrugged his shoulders.

"That fellow he can't speakety English," he explained. "I speakety English very good."

The man smiled knowingly, so it seemed to Roddy, impertinently. Roddy felt uncomfortably convinced that some jest was going on behind his back, and he resented the thought.

"Yes," he began hotly, "and I will bet you *understand* it, too."

THE WHITE MICE

Under the table Peter kicked violently at his ankles.

"Read your letter," he said.

The envelope bore only the name Rodman Forrester. The letter began abruptly and was not signed. It read:

"Willemstad is a small place. Every one in it knows every one else. Therefore, the most conspicuous person in it is the last person to arrive. You are the last person to arrive, and, accordingly, everything you do is noted. That this morning you twice passed the Casa Blanca has been already reported both by those who guard it and by those who spy upon it. If you would bring disaster to those you say you wish to serve, keep on as idiotically as you have begun."

The rebuke, although anonymous, turned Roddy's cheeks a rosy red, but he had sufficient self-control to toss the letter to his companion, and to say carelessly: "He wants us to dine with him."

The waiter, who had been openly listening, moved off in the direction of the kitchen. A moment later Roddy saw him bear a dish to the Venezuelan at the head of the long table, and as he proffered it, the two men whispered eagerly.

When Peter had read the warning he threw

it, face down, upon the table, and with a disturbed countenance pretended to devote his attention to the salad dressing. Roddy was now grinning with pleasure, and made no effort to conceal that fact.

"I wouldn't have missed this," he whispered, "for a week in God's country. Apparently everybody's business is everybody else's business, and every one spies on every one. It's like the island where they were too proud to do their own washing, so everybody took in somebody else's washing."

"Who is it from," interrupted Peter irritably, "the Consul?"

Roddy nodded and laughed.

"You may laugh," protested Peter, "but you don't know. You've been in Venezuela only four months, and Captain Codman's been here eighteen years. These people don't look at things the way we do. We think it's all comic opera, but——"

"They're children," declared Roddy tolerantly, "children trying to frighten you with a mask on. And old man Codman—he's caught it, too. The fact that he's been down here eighteen years is the only thing against him. He's lost his sense of humor. The idea," he exclaimed, "of spying on us and sending us anonymous warnings. Why doesn't he come to the hotel and say what he has to say? Where does he think he is—in Siberia?"

Roddy chuckled and clapped his hands loudly for the waiter. He was pleasantly at ease. The breakfast was to his liking, the orange trees shielded him from the sun, and the wind from the sea stirred the flowering shrubs and filled the air with spicy, pungent odors.

"Perhaps the Consul understands them better than you do," persisted Peter. "These revolutionists——"

"They're a pack of cards," declared Roddy. "As Alice said to the King and Queen, 'You're only a pack of cards.'"

As he was speaking Mr. Von Amberg, the agent of the steamship line, with whom that morning he had been in consultation, and one of the other commission merchants of Willemstad, came up the gravel walk and halted at their table.

Both Von Amberg and his companion had but lately arrived from Holland. They were big men, of generous girth, beaming with good health and good humor. They looked like Kris Kringles in white duck. In continental fashion they raised their Panama hats and bowed profusely. They congratulated the young men on so soon having found their way to the Café Ducrot, and that Mr. de Peyster, whose name appealed to them, had pronounced the cooking excellent, afforded them personal satisfaction.

Von Amberg told the young men he had just left cards for the club at their hotel, and hoped they would make use of it. His launch, carriage and he, himself, were at their disposition.

When Roddy invited the two merchants to join them Von Amberg thanked him politely and explained that his table was already laid for breakfast. With another exchange of bows the two gentlemen continued up the twisting path and disappeared among the bushes.

"*That's* what I mean!" exclaimed Roddy approvingly. "Now they are *our* people. They have better manners, perhaps, than we have, but they're sensible, straight-from-the-shoulder men of business. *They* aren't spying on anybody, or sending black-hand letters, or burying old men alive in prisons. If they saw a revolution coming they wouldn't know what——"

He was interrupted by the sudden reappearance of the men of whom he spoke. They were moving rapidly in the direction of the gate, and the countenance of each wore an expression of surprise and alarm. While his companion passed them quickly, Mr. Von Amberg reluctantly hesitated, and, in evident perplexity and with some suspicion, looked from one to the other. The waiter had placed the coffee and bottles of cognac and of curaçao upon the table; and Roddy hospitably moved a chair forward.

"Won't you change your mind," he said, "and try some of the stuff that made this island famous?"

In spite of his evident desire to escape, Von Amberg's good manners did not forsake him. He bowed and raised his hat in protest.

"I—I should be very pleased—some other time," he stammered, "but now I must return to town. I find to-day it is not possible to breakfast here. There is a large party—" he paused, and his voice rose interrogatively.

"Yes," Roddy replied with indifference. "We found them here. They took all the waiters away from us."

The nature of the answer seemed greatly to surprise Von Amberg.

"You—you are not acquainted with those gentlemen?" he inquired.

In the fashion of his country, Roddy answered by another question.

"Who are they?" he asked. "Who is the one whose health they are all the time drinking?"

For an instant Von Amberg continued to show complete bewilderment. Then he smiled broadly. For him, apparently, the situation now possessed an aspect as amusing as it had been disturbing. He made a sly face and winked jovially.

"Oh! You Americans!" he exclaimed. "You make good politicians. Do not fear," he added hurriedly. "I have seen nothing, and I say nothing. I do not mix myself in politics." He started toward the gate, then halted, and with one eye closed whispered hoarsely, "It is all right. I will say nothing!" Nodding mysteriously, he hurried down the path.

Peter leaned back in his chair and chuckled delightedly.

"There go your sensible business men," he jeered, "running away! Now what have you to say?"

Roddy was staring blankly down the path and shook his head.

"You can subpœna me," he sighed. "Why should they be afraid of a birthday-party? Why!" he exclaimed, "they were even afraid of *me!* He didn't believe that we don't know those Venezuelans. He said," Roddy recapitulated, "he didn't mix in politics. That means, of course, that those fellows are politicians, and, probably this is their fashion of holding a primary. It must be the local method of floating a revolution. But why should Von Am-

THE WHITE MICE

berg think we're in the plot, too? Because my name's Forrester?"

Peter nodded. "That must be it," he said. "Your father is in deep with these Venezuelans, and everybody knows that, and makes the mistake of thinking you are also. I wish," he exclaimed patiently, "your father was more confiding. It is all very well for him—plotting plots from the top of the Forrester Building—but it makes it difficult for any one down here inside the firing-line. If your father isn't more careful," he protested warmly, "Alvarez will stand us blindfolded against a wall, and we'll play blind man's buff with a firing-squad."

Peter's forebodings afforded Roddy much amusement. He laughed at his friend, and mocked him, urging him to keep a better hold upon his sense of humor.

"You have been down here too long yourself," he said. "You'll be having tropic choler next. I tell you, you must think of them as children: they're a pack of cards."

"Maybe they are," sighed Peter; "but as long as we don't know the game——"

From where Peter sat, with his back in their direction, he could not see the Venezuelans; but Roddy, who was facing them, now observed that they had finished their break-

THE WHITE MICE

fast. Talking, gesticulating, laughing, they were crowding down the path. He touched Peter, and Peter turned in his chair to look at them.

At the same moment a man stepped from the bushes, and halting at one side of Roddy, stood with his eyes fixed upon the men of the birthday-party, waiting for them to approach. He wore the silk cap of a chauffeur, a pair of automobile goggles, and a long automobile coat. The attitude of the chauffeur suggested that he had come forward to learn if his employer was among those now making their departure; and Roddy wondered that he had heard no automobile arrive, and that he had seen none in Willemstad. Except for that thought, so interested was Roddy in the men who had shown so keen an interest in him, that to the waiting figure he gave no further consideration.

The Venezuelans had found they were too many to walk abreast. Some had scattered down other paths. Others had spread out over the grass. But the chief guest still kept to the gravel walk which led to the gate. And now Roddy saw him plainly.

Owing to a charming quality of youth, it was impossible to guess the man's age. He might be under thirty. He might be forty.

THE WHITE MICE

He was tall, graceful, and yet soldierly-looking, with crisp, black hair clinging close to a small, aristocratic head. Like many Venezuelans, he had the brown skin, ruddy cheeks, and pointed mustache of a Neapolitan. His eyes were radiant, liquid, brilliant. He was walking between two of his friends, with a hand resting affectionately on the shoulder of each; and though both of the men were older than himself, his notice obviously flattered them. They were laughing, and nodding delighted approval at what he said, and he was talking eagerly and smiling. Roddy thought he had seldom seen a smile so winning, one that carried with it so strong a personal appeal. Roddy altogether approved of the young man. He found him gay, buoyant, in appearance entirely the conquering hero, the Prince Charming. And even though of his charm the young man seemed to be well aware, he appeared none the less a graceful, gallant, triumphant figure.

As Roddy, mildly curious, watched him, the young man turned his head gayly from the friend on his one side to address the one on the other. It was but a movement of an instant, but in the short circuit of the glance Roddy saw the eyes of the young man halt. As though suddenly hypnotized, his lips slowly closed, his white teeth disappeared, the charm-

THE WHITE MICE

ing smile grew rigid. He was regarding something to the left of Roddy and above him.

Roddy turned and saw the waiting figure of the chauffeur. He had stepped clear of the bushes, and, behind the mask-like goggles, his eyes were fixed upon the young Venezuelan. He took a short step forward, and his right hand reached up under his left cuff.

Roddy had seen Englishmen in searching for a handkerchief make a similar movement, but now the gesture was swift and sinister. In the attitude of the masked figure itself there was something prehensible and menacing. The hand of the man came free, and Roddy saw that it held a weapon.

As the quickest way to get his legs from under the table, Roddy shoved the table and everything on it into the lap of Peter. With one spring Roddy was beside the man, and as he struck him on the chin, with his other hand he beat at the weapon. There were two reports and a sharp high cry.

Under the blow the masked man staggered drunkenly, his revolver swaying in front of Roddy's eyes. Roddy clutched at it and there was a struggle—another report—and then the man broke from him, and with the swift, gliding movement of a snake, slipped through the bushes.

Under the blow the masked man staggered drunkenly.

III

Roddy stood staring blankly, unconsciously sucking at a raw spot on his finger where the powder had burned it. At his feet the bottle of curaçao, from which he had just been drinking, was rolling upon the gravel path, its lifeblood bubbling out upon the pebbles. He stooped and lifted it. Later he remembered wondering how it had come there, and, at the time, that so much good liquor had been wasted had seemed a most irritating circumstance.

He moved to replace the bottle upon the table and found the table overturned, with Peter, his clothes dripping and his eyes aflame, emerging from beneath it.

Further up the path the young Venezuelan was struggling in the arms of his friends. Fearful that he might still be in danger they were restraining him, and he, eager to pursue the man who had fired on him, was crying aloud his protests. Others of his friends were racing down the different paths, breaking through the bushes, and often, in their excitement, seizing upon one another. Huddled together in a group, the waiters and coachmen explained, gesticulated, shrieked.

But above the clamor of all, the voice of Peter was the most insistent. Leaping from a wreck of plates and glasses, his clothing splashed with claret, with coffee, with salad dressing, with the tablecloth wound like a kilt about his legs, he jumped at Roddy and Roddy retreated before him. Raging, and in the name of profane places, Peter demanded what Roddy "meant" by it.

"Look at me!" he commanded. "Look what you did! Look at me!"

Roddy did not look. If he looked he knew he would laugh. And he knew Peter was hoping he would laugh so that, at that crowning insult, he might fall upon him.

In tones of humble, acute regret Roddy protested.

"I did it, Peter," he stammered hastily. "I did it—to save you. I was afraid he would hit you. I had to act quickly——"

"Afraid *he'd* hit me!" roared Peter. "*You* hit me! Hit me with a table! Look at my new white flannel suit! And look at this!" With his fingers he gingerly parted his wet, dishevelled hair. "Look at the bump on the back of my head. Is *that* your idea of saving

THE WHITE MICE

me? I wish," he exploded savagely, "I wish he'd shot you full of holes!"

The violent onslaught of Peter was interrupted by one hardly less violent from the young Venezuelan. He had freed himself from his friends, and, as it now was evident the man who had attempted his life had escaped, and that to search further was useless, he ran to thank the stranger who had served him. Extravagantly, but with real feeling, he wrung both of Roddy's hands. In the native fashion he embraced him, shook him by the shoulders, patted him affectionately on the back. Eloquently but incoherently in Spanish, French and English he poured forth his thanks. He hailed Roddy as his preserver, his *bon amigo*, his *brav camarad*. In expressing their gratitude his friends were equally voluble and generous. They praised, they applauded, they admired; in swift, graceful gestures they re-enacted for each other the blow upon the chin, the struggle for the revolver, the escape of the would-be assassin.

Even Peter, as the only one who had suffered, became a heroic figure.

It was many minutes before the Americans could depart, and then only after every one had drunk to them in warm, sweet champagne.

When the glasses were filled the young Venezuelan turned to those standing about him on the grass and commanded silence. He now spoke in excellent English, but Roddy noted that those of the older men who could not understand regarded him with uneasiness.

"I ask you, my friends," cried the Venezuelan, "to drink to the name of Forrester. How much," he exclaimed, "does not that name mean to my unhappy country. I—myself—that *my* life should be taken—it is nothing; but that it should be saved for my country by one of that name is for us an omen—a lucky omen. It means," he cried, the soft, liquid eyes flashing, "it means success. It means—" As though suddenly conscious of the warning frowns of his friends, he paused abruptly, and with a graceful bow, and waving his glass toward Roddy, said quietly, "Let us drink to the son of a good friend of Venezuela—to Mr. Forrester."

Not until the landau was well on its way to Willemstad did Roddy deem it wise to make a certain inquiry.

"What," he asked of the driver, "is the name of the gentleman that the other gentleman tried to shoot?"

The driver turned completely in his seat. His eyes were opened wide in amazement.

"You don't know that gentleman!" he exclaimed. "I think everybody know *that* gentleman. He be very brave Venezuela gentleman; he be Colonel Vega."

As though sure of the effect of that name, the driver paused dramatically, but, except that the two Americans looked inquiringly at each other, they made no sign.

"Mebbe I better call that gentleman—Pino?" the driver suggested. "Everybody call him Pino, just like he be everybody's brother." The man showed his teeth broadly, in a delighted grin. "The market womens, the sailor mens, the police mens, the black peoples, and the white gentlemens, everybodys—call him Pino. Pino he be exiled. If he go to his country that President Alvarez he say he shoot him. So Pino go over that way," with his whip he pointed to the east. "They say he go live in Paris. But yesterday he come in that steamer, and all the peoples be waiting at that wharf. Everybody be glad to see Pino."

"Everybody but that man with that gun," suggested Roddy.

The driver rolled his eyes darkly and pursed his lips. "That be bad man," he said.

"Did President Alvarez," inquired Roddy pleasantly, "send that bad man over here to shoot the too popular Pino?"

THE WHITE MICE

Peter uttered a sudden growl of indignation.

"Look where you are driving!" he ordered. When the negro had turned to his horses Peter stared at Roddy long and steadily.

"What that parrot said of you," he declared grimly, "was true."

Those Venezuelans who at once had set forth on their ponies to overtake the would-be assassin already had brought word of the attempt upon Colonel Vega to Willemstad, and the repose of the peaceful burgh was greatly ruffled. The arrival of the young men increased the excitement, and, though they fled to their rooms, from their balcony overlooking the wharf they could hear their driver, enthroned upon his box seat, describing the event to an intent and eager audience.

As Peter was changing into dry clothes he held his watch so that Roddy could note the hour.

"How long would you have said we have been living on this island?" he asked.

"Oh, at least a week!" exclaimed Roddy. "I have had more excitement than I could get in New York in a year, and we haven't been here twelve hours!"

"But it is all over now," Peter announced. "We can't stay here. We're getting too chummy with this Venezuelan crowd, thanks to you."

"What have I done now?" complained Roddy.

"You can't help being who you are," admitted Peter, "but you can see that this town is a red-hot incubator for revolutions. Every one in it thinks of nothing else, and every one thinks you are in deep with your father against Alvarez, and if we linger here Alvarez will think so, too. We've got to get back to Porto Cabello where we have a clean bill of health."

Roddy had stretched himself upon his cot, in preparation for his afternoon siesta, but he sat upright, his face filled with dismay.

"And not see the Rojas family?" he cried.

Peter growled indignantly.

"See them! How can you see them?" he demanded. "We only drove past their house, along a public road, and already everybody in town has a flashlight picture of us doing it."

"But," objected Roddy, "we haven't got our credentials."

"We'll have to do without them," declared Peter. "I tell you, if you get mixed up with Brother Pino when you get back to Porto Cabello you'll go to jail. And what chance will we have then of saving General Rojas? He will stay in prison and die there. As White

THE WHITE MICE

Mice," announced Peter firmly, "we have our work to do, and we must not be turned aside by anybody's revolution, your father's, or Pino Vega's, or anybody's. We're White Mice, first, last and all the time. Our duty isn't to take life but to save it." As though suddenly surprised by a new idea Peter halted abruptly.

"I suppose," he demanded scornfully, "you think you prevented a murder this morning, and you will be claiming the White Mice medal for saving life?"

"I certainly will," declared Roddy cheerfully, "and you will have to certify I earned it, because you saw me earn it."

"But I didn't," declared Peter. "I was under the table."

Roddy closed his eyes and again fell back upon the cot. For so long a time was he silent that Peter, who had gone out upon the balcony, supposed him asleep, when Roddy suddenly raised himself on his elbow.

"Anyway," he began abruptly, "we can't leave here until the boat takes us away, three days from now. I'll bet in three days I'll get all the credentials we want."

Roddy had been awake since sunrise, the heat was soporific, the events of the morning exhausting, and in two minutes, unmindful of revolutions, indifferent to spies, to plots and counter-plots, he was sleeping happily. But as he slumbered, in two lands, at great distances apart, he and his affairs were being earnestly considered. On the twenty-seventh floor of the Forrester Building his father, with perplexed and frowning brows, studied a cablegram; in the Casa Blanca, Señora Rojas and her daughters listened in amazement to a marvellous tale. Had it not been their faithful friend and jealous guardian, the American Consul, who was speaking, they could not have credited it.

At the Forrester Building the cablegram had been just translated from the secret code of the company and placed upon the desk of Mr. Forrester. It was signed by Von Amberg, and read: "To-day at meeting your party, unknown man fired three shots Vega; Young Forrester overpowered man; Vega unhurt; man escaped. Understand young Forrester not in our confidence. Please instruct."

Three times Mr. Forrester read the cablegram, and then, laying it upon his knee, sat staring out of the open window.

Before his physical eyes were deep canyons of office buildings like his own, towering crag above crag, white curling columns of smoke from busy tugboats, and the great loom of the Brooklyn Bridge with its shuttles of clattering

THE WHITE MICE

cable-cars. But what he saw was his son, alone in a strange land, struggling with an unknown man, a man intent on murder. With a hand that moved unsteadily the Lighthouse King lifted the desk telephone and summoned the third vice-president, and when Mr. Sam Caldwell had entered, silently gave him the cablegram.

Sam Caldwell read it and exclaimed with annoyance:

"Looks to me," he commented briskly, "as though they know why Pino came back. Looks as though they had sent this fellow to do him up, before we can——"

In a strange, thin voice, Mr. Forrester stopped him sharply.

"If the boy'd been hurt—they'd have said so, wouldn't they?" he demanded.

Sam Caldwell recognized his error. Carefully he reread the cablegram.

"Why, of course," he assented heartily. "It says here he overpowered the other fellow: says 'Vegas unhurt.'"

In the same unfamiliar, strained tone Mr. Forrester interrupted. "It doesn't say Roddy is unhurt," he objected.

The young man laughed reassuringly.

"But the very fact they don't say so shows—why, they'd know that's what you most want to hear. I wouldn't worry about Roddy. Not for a minute."

Embarrassed by his own feeling, annoyed that Sam Caldwell should have discovered it, Mr. Forrester answered, "*You* wouldn't. He isn't *your* son."

He reached for a cable form, and wrote rapidly:

"Von Amberg. Willemstad, Curaçao, W. I. Forrester most certainly not in our confidence. Return him Cabello. Is he"—the pen hesitated and then again moved swiftly—"unhurt?"

He drew another blank toward him and addressing it to McKildrick, wrote: "Why is Forrester in Curaçao? Cable him return. Keep him on job, or lose yours."

For a moment Mr. Forrester sat studying the two messages, then he raised his eyes.

"I have half a mind," he said, "to order him home. I would, if he weren't doing so well down there." With an effort to eliminate from his voice any accent of fatherly pride, Mr. Forrester asked coldly: "McKildrick reports that he is doing well, doesn't he?"

The third vice-president nodded affirmatively.

"If he comes back here," argued Mr. Forrester, "he'll do nothing but race his car, and he'll learn nothing of the business. And then, again," he added doubtfully, "while he's down

THE WHITE MICE

there I don't want him to learn too much of the business, not this Pino Vega end of it, or he might want to take a hand, and that might embarrass us. Perhaps I had better cable him, too."

He looked inquiringly at the third vice-president, but that gentleman refused to be drawn.

"He isn't *my* son," he remarked.

"I am not speaking of him as my son," snapped Mr. Forrester warmly. "Speaking of him, not as my son, but as an employee of the company, what would *you* do with him?"

"I'd cable him to mind his own business," answered Sam Caldwell.

For the fraction of a second, under levelled eyebrows, Mr. Forrester stared at young Mr. Caldwell, and then, as a sign that the interview was at an end, swung in his swivel chair and picked up his letters. Over his shoulder he said, "Cable him that."

While Roddy in Willemstad was slumbering under his mosquito-net, and Sam Caldwell in New York was concocting a cablegram, which, he calculated, would put Roddy in his proper place, but which, instead, put him in a very bad temper, Captain Codman, at Casa Blanca, had just finished relating his marvellous tale.

THE WHITE MICE

It was the story of how young Forrester, without letters of introduction, without credentials, had that morning walked into the Consulate and announced that, without asking advice, he intended to liberate the Lion of Valencia.

Upon the members of the Rojas household the marvellous tale had a widely different effect.

To understand why this should be so it is necessary to know something of the three women who formed the Rojas household.

Señora Rojas was an American. When she was very young her father, a professor at one of the smaller universities in New England, in order to study the archives of the Spanish rulers of Venezuela had visited that country, and taken his daughter with him. She was spirited, clever, and possessed of the particular type of beauty the Spaniard admires. Young Rojas saw her, and at once fell in love with her, and, after the death of her father, which occurred in the North, followed her there and married her. She then was very young and he an attaché in the diplomatic service. Since their marriage, unlike many of his countrymen, Rojas had not looked with interest upon any other woman, and, with each year of their life together, their affection had grown stronger, their dependence upon each other had increased.

THE WHITE MICE

In wisdom, in experience, in honors, Rojas had grown rich. In countries where his own was only a spot upon the map, Rojas himself, the statesman, the diplomat, the man who spoke and read in many languages, the charming host with the brilliant wife, was admired, sought after. There were three children: the two girls, and a son, a lieutenant of artillery, whose death during the revolution of Andreda had brought to the family its first knowledge of grief.

Of the two sisters, Lolita, the elder, was like her father—grave, gracious, speaking but seldom and, in spite of the years spent in foreign capitals, still a Spanish-American. Her interests were in her church, her music and the duties of the household.

Of all the names given at her christening to the younger sister, the one that survived was Inez. Inez was a cosmopolitan. She had been permitted to see too much of the world to make it possible for her ever again to sit down tamely behind the iron bars of the Porto Cabello drawing-room. She was too much like her American mother; not as her mother was now, after thirty years in a Venezuelan's household, but as her mother had been when she left the New England college town. Unlike her sister, she could not be satisfied with the cloister-like life

THE WHITE MICE

of the young girls of Spanish-America. During the time her father had served as minister to Paris she had been at school in the convent at Neuilly, but at the time he was transferred to London she was of an age to make her bow at court, and old enough to move about with a freedom which, had it been permitted her at home, would have created public scandal. She had been free to ride in the Row, to play tennis, to walk abroad, even through public streets and parks, even when it rained, even unattended. She had met men, not always as prospective suitors, but as friends and companions.

And there had been a wonderful visit to her mother's country and her mother's people, when for a summer she had rejoiced in the friendly, inconsequent, out-of-door life of a Massachusetts seaside colony. Once on the North Shore, and later on Cape Cod, she had learned to swim, to steer a knockabout, to dance the "Boston," even in rubber-soled shoes, to "sit out" on the Casino balcony and hear young men, with desperate anxiety, ask if there were any more in South America like her. To this question she always replied that there were not; and that, in consequence, if the young man had any thoughts on the subject, she was the person to whom they should be addressed.

Then, following the calm, uneventful life of

the convent, of London and its gayeties, of the Massachusetts coast with its gray fogs and open, driftwood fires, came the return to her own country. There, with her father, she rode over his plantations among the wild cattle, or with her mother and sister sat in the *patio* and read novels in three languages, or sleepily watched the shadow of the tropical sun creep across the yellow wall.

And then, suddenly, all of these different, happy lives were turned into memories, shadows, happenings of a previous and unreal existence. There came a night, which for months later in terrified dreams returned to haunt her, a night when she woke to find her bed surrounded by soldiers, to hear in the court-yard the sobs of her mother and the shrieks of the serving-women, to see her father —concerned only for his wife and daughters— in a circle of the secret police, to see him, before she could speak with him, hurried to a closed carriage and driven away.

Then had begun the two years of exile in Willemstad, the two years of mourning, not of quiet grief for one at rest, but anxious, unending distress for one alive, one dearly loved, one tortured in mind, enduring petty indignities, bodily torments, degradations that killed the soul and broke the brave spirit.

THE WHITE MICE

To the three women Rojas had been more than husband or father. He had been their knight, their idol, their reason for happiness. They alone knew how brave he was, how patient, how, beyond imagination, considerate. That they should be free to eat and sleep, to work and play, while he was punished like a felon, buried alive, unable to carry on the work in the world God had given him to do, caused them intolerable misery. While he suffered there was no taste in life, and the three shut themselves from the world. They admitted only the Consul, who had been his friend, and those who, like themselves, were exiles, and in whose hatred of Alvarez lay their only hope of again seeing the one they loved. Time after time a plan of rescue had failed. A plot that promised release had been disclosed and the conspirators punished. Hope had left them, and, on the part of their friends, had been followed by lethargy.

But within the last three months a new hope had arisen, and with it, for the younger daughter, a new distress.

It was whispered that a revolution, backed by great wealth and sanctified by the prayers of the people, was to be started near Valencia. Its leader in the field was to be young Pino Vega, in several campaigns the personal aide-de-camp

THE WHITE MICE

of General Rojas, a young man indebted to his chief for many favors, devoted to him by reason of mutual confidence and esteem. If successful, this revolt against Alvarez was to put Vega in command of the army, to free Rojas and to place him as president at Miraflores. To the women the thought that Rojas might become president was intolerable. It was because he had consented to be president that he had suffered. The mere thought of the office, and of the cruelties that had been practised by the man who held it, made it, to the women, terrifying.

For Rojas they wanted neither position nor power. They wanted Rojas free. They wanted to hold him close, to touch him, to look into his eyes, to see the gentle, understanding smile.

Each felt that there was nothing she could not do, no sacrifice she would not make, if once more she could sit beside him, holding his hand, waiting in silence for the joy of hearing him speak. And of the younger girl the sacrifice has been required. At least a way in which she could assist the cause that would lead to the freedom of her father had been presented to her. From Paris, Pino Vega had written her mother, requesting permission to ask Inez to be his wife.

To the girl, of all the men she knew in Venezuela, Pino was the most attractive. They both had lived for years outside of their own country and, in consequence, had much in common. He was thirty-seven, older than she by fourteen years, but, as has already been pointed out, in appearance, in manner, in spirits, he seemed much younger than his years. To his detriment nothing could be said that could not have been said of the other young men of his class in his country. But the girl was not in love with the young man of that class, nor with her country.

Her brother had been sacrificed in what to her had seemed but a squalid struggle for place between two greedy politicians; her father, for the very reason that he had served his country loyally, faithfully, and was, in consequence, beloved by the people, had been caged like a wild animal. She had no love for her native land. She distrusted and feared it.

Night after night, as she paced the walk along the cliff where the waves broke at her feet, she shuddered to think of returning to that land, only sixty miles from her, that had robbed her of so much that had made life beautiful; of all, up to the present, that had made it happy. She wished never to see it again. Could her father have been returned to her she would have rejoiced that they were exiles. And, as she distrusted the country, she distrusted the men of the country, at least those of the class to which Vega belonged. She knew them well, the born orators, born fighters, born conspirators. To scheme, to plot, to organize against the authority of the moment was in their blood.

If she thought of a possible husband, and, in a country where a girl marries at fifteen, and where her first, if not her only duty in life, is to marry, it would have been surprising if she had not, the man she considered as a husband was not a Venezuelan. For their deference to women, for their courtesy to each other, for their courage as shown in their campaigns, for their appreciation of art, of letters, of music, she greatly admired her countrymen; but that they themselves created nothing, that they scorned labor and all those who labored, made them, to Inez, intolerable.

That she was half an American of the North was to her a source of secret pride. With satisfaction she remembered young men she had known during the summers on the North Shore and Cape Cod, the young men who, during the first of the week, toiled and sweltered in their offices, and who, when the week-end came, took their pleasures strenuously, in exercise and sport. She liked to remember that her American and English devotees had treated

THE WHITE MICE

her as a comrade, as an intelligent, thinking creature. They had not talked to her exclusively of the beauty of her eyes, her teeth and hair.

She preferred their breathless, "Well played, partner!" to the elaborate, "I saw the Señorita at mass this morning. As she raised her eyes to Heaven—the angels grew jealous."

When the mother told Inez that Colonel Vega had written, proposing on his return to pay his addresses to her, the girl was in genuine distress. She protested earnestly.

In thirty years Señora Rojas unconsciously had assimilated the thoughts, the habits, the attitude of mind of the women of her adopted country, and, when Inez had finished her protests, her mother, seeing the consequence from her own point of view, was greatly disturbed. "It is most unfortunate," she said. "Pino is selfish; when he learns you will not listen to him he will be very angry and he will be less eager to help your father. He will think only of himself. If you only could have cared——"

"Pino could not be so cruel," said the girl. But she spoke as though she were arguing against her own conviction. "He cannot be so vain—so spoiled," she protested, "that because one woman fails to fall on her knees to him, he must punish her."

THE WHITE MICE

The talk between the mother and daughter had taken place a week before Colonel Vega's arrival from Paris. On the day his steamer was due, Señora Rojas again spoke to Inez.

"After mass this morning," she said, "I consulted Father Paul about Pino. He hopes it will be possible for you not to give him a direct answer. He says Pino will be leaving us almost at once. He is to land north of Porto Cabello, and our people are to join him there. Father Paul thinks," the Señora hesitated, and then went on hastily, "you might let him go in ignorance. You might ask for time to consider. You might even tell him——"

The girl's cheeks flushed crimson and the tears came to her eyes. The mother looked away. After an instant's silence she exclaimed bitterly: "It is only a lie to a man who has lied to many women! I think of nothing," she declared, "but that it would keep him true to your father. What else matters!" she broke forth, "I would lie, cheat, steal," she cried, "if I could save your father one moment's suffering."

The girl took the hand of the elder woman and pressed it to her cheek. "I know," she whispered, "I know."

There was a moment's silence. "If it were anything else!" protested the girl. "If I could change places with father I would run to do it —you know that—but this"—with a gesture of repugnance the girl threw out her hands— "to pretend—to care! It is degrading, it makes me feel unclean."

"You will make an enemy," asked the mother coldly, "of the only person who can bring your father back to us? Sooner than let Pino think you care for him, you would let him turn against us? You and Pino," she pleaded, "are old friends. Your father is his friend. What more natural!" She broke forth hysterically. "I beg of you," she cried, "I command you not to make an enemy of Pino. Tell him to wait, tell him that now you can think of nothing but your father, but that when your father is free, that if he will only set him free—" The mother held the girl toward her, searching her eyes. "Promise me," she begged.

Inez regarded her mother unhappily, and turned away.

This, then, on the afternoon of Colonel Vega's arrival at Curaçao was the position toward him and toward each other of the three women of the Rojas household, and explains, perhaps, why, when that same afternoon Captain Codman told them the marvellous tale of Roddy's proposition, Señora Rojas and her daughter received the news each in a different manner.

THE WHITE MICE

Before she had fully understood, Señora Rojas exclaimed with gratitude:

"It is the hand of God. It is His hand working through this great company."

"Not at all," snapped Captain Codman. "The company has nothing to do with it. As far as I can see it is only the wild plan of a harum-scarum young man. He has no authority. He's doing it for excitement, for an adventure. He doesn't seem to know anything of —of what is going on—and, personally, I think he's mad. He and his friend are the two men who twice drove past your house this morning. What his friend is like I don't know; but Forrester seems quite capable of forcing his way in here. He wants what he calls 'credentials.' In fact, when I refused to help him, he as much as threatened to come here and get them for himself."

The voice of Señora Rojas was shaken with alarm. "He is coming here!" she cried. "But if he is seen *here* they will know at once at Caracas, and my husband will suffer. It may mean the end of everything." Her voice rose, trembling with indignation. "How dare he! How dare he, for the sake of an adventure, risk the life of my husband? How can he expect to succeed where our friends have failed, and now, when Pino has returned and there is hope."

THE WHITE MICE

"I told him that," said the Consul.

"You warned him," insisted the Señora; "you told him he must not come near us?"

Inez, who, with her sister, stood eagerly intent behind the chair in which their mother was seated, laid her hand soothingly upon the Señora's shoulder.

"Is it best," she asked, "to turn the young man away without learning what he wishes to do? Living in Porto Cabello, he may know something we could not know. Did you find out," she asked the Consul, "in what way Mr. Forrester wishes to help us?"

"No," confessed Captain Codman, "I did not. I was so taken aback," he explained; "he was so ignorant, so cocksure, that he made me mad. And I just ordered him out, and I told him, told him for his own good, of course," the Consul added hastily, "that he talked too much."

With critical eyes Inez regarded her old friend doubtfully, and shook her head at him.

"And how did he take that?" she asked.

"He told me," answered the Consul, painfully truthful, "that my parrot had said the same thing, and that we might both be wrong."

There was an instant's silence, and then Inez laughed. In shocked tones her mother exclaimed reprovingly.

"But he comes here," protested the girl, "to do us a service, the greatest service, and he is ordered away. Why should we refuse to let him help us, to let any one help us. We should make the most of every chance that offers."

Señora Rojas turned in her chair and looked steadily at her daughter.

"Your advice is good, Inez," she said, "but it comes strangely from you."

At the same moment, as though conjured by her thought, a servant announced Colonel Vega, and that gentleman, with several of those who had lunched with him at the Café Ducrot, entered the room. In alarm Captain Codman waited only to shake hands with the visitors and then precipitately departed. But in the meeting of the exiles there was nothing that would have compromised him. The reception of Colonel Vega by the three women was without outward significance. They greeted him, not as a leader of their conspiracy, but as they might have received any friend who, after an absence, had returned to them. When he bent over the hand of Inez he raised his liquid eyes to hers, but the girl welcomed him simply, without confusion.

He decided that her mother could not as yet have told her of his wishes. Had she done so he felt sure, in view of the honor he would

THE WHITE MICE

pay her, her embarrassment at meeting him would have been apparent to all.

Vega himself elected to tell the ladies of the attack made upon him at the Café Ducrot. He made little of it. He let the ladies understand that his life, like that of all public men, was always at the mercy of assassins. To Roddy he gave full credit.

"Imagine this man reaching for his weapon," he related dramatically, "myself too far from him to fall upon him, and my arms resting upon the shoulders of my two good friends. Their safety, also, is in my mind. But I am helpless. I saw the villain smile confidently. He points the weapon. Then the young man springs upon him and the bullets pass us harmlessly. Believe me, but for Mr. Forrester all three of us, General Pulido, Colonel Ramon and myself, might now be dead."

The two gentlemen designated dismissed the thought with a negligent wave of the hand. It suggested that, to soldiers like themselves, being dead was an annoyance to which they had grown accustomed.

"Mr. Forrester!" exclaimed Inez, catching at the name.

"Mr. Forrester!" repeated her mother. "But I thought—I was told only just now that he knew nothing of our plans."

"That is quite true," Colonel Vega assured her. "He was not with us. He was there by accident."

"Let us rather say," corrected Señora Rojas piously, "he was placed there by a special Providence to save you."

That the Almighty should be especially concerned in his well-being did not appear to Vega as at all unlikely.

He nodded his head gravely.

"It may be so," he admitted.

Through force of habit Señora Rojas glanced about her; but the open windows showed the empty garden, and around her, seated in two rows of rocking-chairs, the ladies facing the door, the men facing the ladies, she saw only friends.

"But why," she asked, "is young Mr. Forrester *not* in the confidence of his father? Can he not trust his own son?"

As though sure of her answer she cast a triumphant glance at the daughter who had dared, against Captain Codman and herself, to champion Mr. Forrester's son. Pino frowned mysteriously. He did not like to say that with any action of the great Mr. Forrester he was not acquainted. So he scowled darkly and shook his head.

"It is a puzzle," he said; "the young man is

THE WHITE MICE

a fine fellow. To him I owe my life." He appealed to his friends, who, in time to the sedate rocking of the chairs, nodded gravely. "But his father is very decided. He cables us to send him at once to Porto Cabello. He instructs us not to let him know what we plan to do. I learned that in Porto Cabello he is only a workman, or, a little better, the foreman of the Jamaica coolies. I do not say so," Pino pointed out, as though if he wished he might say a great deal, "but it looks as though he were here for some punishment—as though he had displeased his father. Or," he demanded, "why should his father, who is so wealthy, give his son the wages of a foreman?"

During the visit of the conspirators the traditions of Spanish etiquette gave Colonel Vega no opportunity to separate Inez from the others; and soon, without having spoken to her alone, he and his followers departed.

When they had gone, Inez, as was her custom when she wished to be by herself, ordered her pony and rode out on the cliff road toward the orange groves. Riding unattended was a breach of Spanish-American convention. But her mother permitted it, and, in the eyes of the people of Willemstad, her long residence abroad, and the fact that she was half American of the North, partially excused it. Every

THE WHITE MICE

morning at sunrise, before the heat of the day, and just before the sun set, Inez made these excursions. They were the bright moments of her present life. If she did not wish to think, they prevented her from thinking; if she did wish to think, they protected her from intrusion, and gave her strength and health to bear the grinding anxiety of the other hours. They brought back to her, also, memories of rides of former days, before her father had been taken from her, when they had trotted politely over the tan bark of Rotten Row, or when, with her soldier brother, she had chased the wild cattle on the plantation.

Now, with her head bent, with the hand that held the reins lying loosely on her knee, she rode at a walk, her body relaxed, her eyes seeing nothing. Her mind was intent upon her problem, one in which her answer to Pino Vega was but a part. To carry out the plan she had in mind she needed a man to help her, and there were two men to whom she might appeal. But only one, not both of them, could help her. She was determined not to return from her ride until she had decided which one it should be.

After an hour, as though she had reached her decision and was fearful lest she might reconsider it, she lifted the pony into a gallop

THE WHITE MICE

and raced to Casa Blanca. On arriving there she went directly to her room, wrote a note, and returned with it to the stable where the groom was just removing the saddle from her pony.

He was an old man, trusted by Inez. As a body servant he had first served her brother, then her father, and after the imprisonment of General Rojas, had volunteered to follow the women of the family into exile. For a moment the girl regarded him earnestly.

"Pedro," she asked, "what would you do to save the master?"

When the man was assured he had understood her he lowered the saddle to the ground, and standing erect threw out his arms with his open palms toward her. In pantomime he seemed to signify that for the purpose she named, his body, his life was at her disposition.

Inez showed him the note.

"You will take this," she said, "to an American, Mr. Forrester. He is at one of the hotels. No one must know you are seeking him, no one must see you give him this note. Not even my mother must suspect that any message has been sent from this house to that gentleman. When he has read the note he will say 'yes' or 'no.' If he asks questions you will

THE WHITE MICE

shake your head. As soon as you get your answer come directly to me."

She gave him the note and after an impressive delay continued: "There is a new plan to save my father. If you deliver this note safely you will have taken the first step to set him free. If you blunder, if it is found out that Mr. Forrester and one of the Rojas family are conspiring together, it will mean greater cruelties for my father; it may mean his death."

The girl had spoken in the way she knew would best appeal to the man before her. And she was not disappointed. His eyes shone with excitement. That he was conspiring, that he was a factor in a plot, that the plot had in view the end he so much desired, filled him with pleasure and pride. Crossing himself he promised to carry out her orders.

As Inez returned to the main portion of the house the sun was just sinking into the sea; and, to keep their daily tryst, her mother and sister were moving toward the cliff. While the crimson disk descended, the three women stood silent and immovable, the face of each turned toward the rim of the horizon. As though her eyes could pierce the sixty miles that lay between her and her father Inez leaned forward, her fingers interlaced, her lips slightly apart. That, at that moment, he was thinking of her, that he

THE WHITE MICE

was looking to where he knew she was on guard, and thinking of him, moved her as greatly as though the daily ceremony was for the first time being carried forward. A wandering breeze, not born of the sea, but of the soil, of tropical plants and forests, and warm with sunshine, caressed her face. It came from the land toward which her eyes were turned. It was comforting, sheltering, breathing of peace. As it touched her she smiled slightly. She accepted it as a good omen, as a message sent from across the sea, to tell her that in the step she had taken she had done well.

IV

AFTER their dinner at the hotel, Roddy and Peter strolled down the quay and over the tiny drawbridge that binds Otrabanda to Willemstad. There, for some time, half-way between the two towns, they loitered against the railing of the bridge, smoking and enjoying the cool night breeze from the sea. After his long nap Roddy was wakeful. He had been told that Willemstad boasted of a *café chantant*, and he was for finding it. But Peter, who had been awake since the ship's steward had aroused him before sunrise, doubted that there was a *café chantant*, and that if it did exist it could keep him from sleep, and announced his determination to seek his bed.

Left to himself, Roddy strolled slowly around the narrow limits of the town. A few of the shops and two of the cafés were still open, throwing bright spaces of light across the narrow sidewalks, but the greater number of houses were tightly barred; the streets slumbered in darkness. For a quarter of an hour Roddy sauntered idly, and then awoke to the fact that he was not alone. Behind him in the shadow, a man with his face hidden in a shawl, the sound of his footsteps muffled by his rope sandals, was following his wanderings.

Under the circumstances, after the developments of the day, Roddy was not surprised, nor was he greatly interested. Even in Porto Cabello, at one time or another, every one was beset by spies. And that here, in the central office of the revolutionists, Alvarez should be well represented was but natural.

Twice, softly and quickly, the man who followed had approached him from the rear, and each time, lest he should have some more serious purpose than to simply spy upon him, Roddy had stepped into the street. But when for the third time the man drew near, his approach was so swift that Roddy had no time to move away. The man brushed against him, and when he had passed Roddy found a letter had been pressed into his hand.

The hour was late, Roddy looked like a tourist, the note had been delivered covertly. Roddy concluded it contained an invitation to some disreputable adventure, and after calling the man the name associated with what Roddy believed to be his ancient and dishonorable profession, he tossed the note into the street.

With a cry of dismay the man ran toward it, but Roddy was before him. As the note had left his hand his fingers had touched upon heavy, waxen seals.

In an instant he had retrieved the note, and, followed eagerly by the man, carried it to the light of a gas lamp. The envelope was not illuminating, the sealing-wax was stamped with no crest or initials, the handwriting was obviously disguised.

After observing that from the shadow the man still watched him, while at the same time he kept an anxious lookout up and down the street, Roddy opened the note. It read: "You have come to Curaçao for a purpose. One who has the success of that purpose most at heart desires to help you. To-morrow, just before sunrise, walk out the same road over which you drove to-day. Beyond the Café Ducrot the bearer of this letter will wait for you with a led horse. Follow him. If you think he is leading you into danger, order him to ride in advance, and cover him with your revolver. If you will come, say to the bearer, '*Vengo*,' if not, '*No vengo*.' He has orders not to reply to any questions of yours. If you speak of this to others, or if the bearer of this suspects you have arranged for others to follow you, he will only lead you back to your hotel, and your chance to right a great wrong will have passed."

THE WHITE MICE

There was no signature. But as though it were an afterthought, at the bottom of the page was written, "Adventures are for the adventurous."

Standing well in the light of the street lamp, with his back to the houses, with his face toward the waiting messenger, Roddy read the letter three times. But after the first reading his eyes neglected the body of the note and raced to the postscript. That was the line that beckoned and appealed; to him it seemed that whoever wrote the letter doubted he would come to the rendezvous, and was by that line enticing him, mocking him, daring him to refuse. It held forth both a promise and a challenge.

As to who the writer of the note might be, there were in Roddy's mind three explanations. He considered them hastily. Peter was the author of the note, and it was a poor joke intended to test him. It was a genuine offer from some one who had guessed the object of his visit to Curaçao and honestly wished to be of service. It came from the man in the mask and his associates, who, resenting his interference of the morning, had pleasant thoughts of luring him down a lonely road and leaving him lying there. Which of the three suppositions might be correct it was impossible to know, but the postscript decided him. He beckoned to the messenger, and the man ran eagerly forward. "I will come," said Roddy. The man smiled with pleasure, bowed to him, and dived into the darkness. As he ran down the street Roddy stood listening until the soft patter of the sandals had ceased, and then slowly returned to the hotel.

For an hour, still speculating as to who his anonymous friend might be, he stood, smoking, upon the balcony. On the quay below him a negro policeman dozed against a hawser-post. A group of cargadores, stretched at length upon stacks of hides, chattered in drowsy undertones. In the moonlight the lamps on the fishing-boats and on the bridge, now locked against the outside world, burned mistily, and the deck of the steamer moored directly below him was as deserted and bare, as uncanny and ghostlike, as the deck of the ship of the Ancient Mariner. Except for the chiming of ships' bells, the whisper of the running tide, and the sleepy murmur of the longshoremen, the town of Willemstad was steeped in sleep and silence. Roddy, finding he could arrive at no satisfactory explanation of the note, woke the night porter, and telling that official he was off before daybreak to shoot wild pigeons, and wanted his coffee at that hour, betook himself to his cot. It seemed as though

THE WHITE MICE

he had not twice tossed on the pillow before the night-watchman stood yawning at his side.

Roddy and Peter occupied adjoining rooms, and the door between the two was unlocked. When Roddy had bathed, dressed, and, with a feeling of some importance, stuck his revolver into his pocket, he opened the door, and, still suspicious that his faithful friend was sending him on a wild-goose chase, for a few moments stood beside his bed. But Peter, deep in the sleep of innocence, was breathing evenly, stentoriously. Not without envying him the hours of rest still before him, Roddy helped himself to Peter's revolver, left him a line saying it was he who had borrowed it, and went out into the dark and empty streets.

Half awake and with his hunger only partially satisfied, Roddy now regarded his expedition with little favor. He reverted strongly to the theory that some one was making a fool of him. He reminded himself that if in New York he had received such a note, he either would have at once dismissed it as a hoax or turned it over to the precinct station-house. But as the darkness changed to gray, and the black bulk of the Café Ducrot came into view, his interest quickened. He encouraged himself with the thought that while in New York

THE WHITE MICE

the wording of the note would be improbable, hysterical, melodramatic, in hot, turbulent Venezuela it was in keeping with the country and with the people.

Since setting forth from the hotel a half hour had passed, and as he left the Café Ducrot behind him the night faded into the gray-blue mist of dawn. Out of the mist, riding slowly toward him, mounted on one pony and leading another, Roddy saw the man who on the night before had brought him the letter. He was leaning forward, peering through the uncertain light. When he recognized Roddy he galloped to him, and with evident pleasure but without speaking, handed him the reins of the led pony. Then motioning to Roddy to wait, he rode rapidly down the road over which the American had just come. Roddy settled himself in the saddle, and with a smile of satisfaction beamed upon the ghostlike world around him. So far, at least, the adventure promised to be genuine. Certainly, he argued, Peter could not have prepared a joke so elaborate.

Apparently satisfied that Roddy had brought no one with him, the messenger now rejoined him, and with a gesture of apology took the lead, and at a smart trot started in the same direction in which Roddy had been walking.

Roddy gave his guide a start of fifty feet,

and followed. With the idea of a possible ambush still in his mind, he held the pony well in hand, and in front of him, in his belt, stuck one of the revolvers. He now was fully awake. No longer in the darkness was he stumbling on foot over the stones and ruts of the road. Instead, the day was breaking and he had under him a good horse, on which, if necessary, he could run away. The thought was comforting, and the sense of possible danger excited him delightfully. When he remembered Peter, sleeping stolidly and missing what was to come, he felt a touch of remorse. But he had been warned to bring no one with him, and of the letter to speak to no one. He would tell Peter later. But, he considered, what if there should be nothing to tell, or, if there were, what if he should not be alive to tell it? If the men who had planned to assassinate Colonel Vega intended to punish him for his interference, they could not have selected a place or hour better suited to their purpose. In all the world, apparently, he was the only soul awake. On either side of him were high hedges of the Spanish bayonet, and back of them acres of orange groves. The homes of the planters lay far from the highway, and along the sides of the road there were no houses, no lodge gates, not even a peon's thatched hut.

THE WHITE MICE

Roddy was approaching a sharp turn in the road, a turn to the left at almost right angles. It was marked by an impenetrable hedge. Up to now, although the hedges would have concealed a regiment, the white road itself had stretched before him, straight and open. But now the turn shut it from his sight. The guide had reached the corner. Instead of taking it, he turned in his saddle and pulled his pony to a walk.

To Roddy the act seemed significant. It was apparent that they had arrived at their rendezvous. Sharply, Roddy also brought his pony to a walk, and with a heavy pull on the reins moved slowly forward. The guide drew to the right and halted. To Roddy's excited imagination this manœuvre could have but one explanation. The man was withdrawing himself from a possible line of fire. Shifting the reins to his left hand, Roddy let the other fall upon his revolver. Holding in the pony and bending forward, Roddy peered cautiously around the corner.

What he saw was so astonishing, so unlike what he expected, so utterly out of place, that, still leaning forward, still with his hand on his revolver, he stared stupidly.

For half a mile the road lay empty, but directly in front of him, blocking the way, was a

Shifting the reins to his left hand, Roddy let the other fall upon his revolver.

THE WHITE MICE

restless, pirouetting pony, and seated upon the pony, unmoved either by his gyrations or by the appearance of a stranger in her path, was a young girl.

As Roddy had cautiously made his approach he had in his mind a picture of skulking Venezuelans with pointed carbines; his ears were prepared for a command to throw up his hands, for the slap of a bullet. He had convinced himself that around the angle of the impenetrable hedge this was the welcome that awaited him. And when he was confronted by a girl who apparently was no more a daughter of Venezuela than she was a masked highwayman, his first thought was that this must be some innocent foreigner stumbling in upon the ambush. In alarm for her safety his eyes searched the road beyond her, the hedges on either side. If she remained for an instant longer he feared she might be the witness to a shocking tragedy, that she herself might even become a victim. But the road lay empty, in the hedges of spiked cactus not a frond stirred; and the aged man who had led him to the rendezvous sat motionless, watchful but undisturbed.

Roddy again turned to the girl and found her closely observing him. He sank back in his saddle and took off his hat. Still scanning the hedges, he pushed his pony beside hers and spoke quickly.

"Pardon me," he said, "but I think you had better ride on. Some men are coming here. They—they may be here now."

That his anxiety was entirely on her account was obvious. The girl colored slightly, and smiled. As she smiled, Roddy for the first time was looking directly at her, and as he looked his interest in assassins and his anxiety as to what they might do passed entirely from him. For months he had not seen a girl of his own people, and that this girl was one of his own people he did not question. Had he first seen her on her way to mass, with a lace shawl across her shoulders, with a high comb and mantilla, he would have declared her to be Spanish, and of the highest type of Spanish beauty. Now, in her linen riding-skirt and mannish coat and stock, with her hair drawn back under a broad-brimmed hat of black straw, she reminded him only of certain girls with whom he had cantered along the Ocean Drive at Newport or under the pines of Aiken. How a young woman so habited had come to lose herself in a lonely road in Curaçao was incomprehensible. Still, it was not for him to object. That the gods had found fit to send her there was, to Roddy, sufficient in itself, and he was extremely grateful. But that fact

THE WHITE MICE

was too apparent. Though he was unconscious of it, the pleasure in his eyes was evident. He still was too startled to conceal his admiration.

The girl frowned, her slight, boyish figure grew more erect.

"My name is Rojas," she said. "My father is General Rojas. I was told you wished to help him, and last night I sent you a note asking you to meet me here."

She spoke in even, matter-of-fact tones. As she spoke she regarded Roddy steadily. When, the night before, Inez had sent the note, she had been able only to guess as to what manner of man it might be with whom she was making a rendezvous at daybreak, in a lonely road. And she had been more than anxious. Now that she saw him she recognized the type and was reassured. But that he was worthy of the secret she wished to confide in him she had yet to determine. As she waited for him to disclose himself she was to all outward appearances tranquilly studying him. But inwardly her heart was trembling, and it was with real relief that, when she told him her name, she saw his look of admiration disappear, and in his eyes come pity and genuine feeling.

"Oh!" gasped Roddy unhappily, his voice filled with concern. "Oh, I am sorry!"

The girl slightly inclined her head.

THE WHITE MICE

"I came to ask you," she began, speaking with abrupt directness, "what you propose to do?"

It was a most disconcerting question. Not knowing what he proposed to do, Roddy, to gain time, slipped to the ground and, hat in hand, moved close to the pommel of her saddle. As he did not answer, the girl spoke again, this time in a tone more kindly. "And to ask why you wish to help us?"

As though carefully considering his reply, Roddy scowled, but made no answer. In a flash it had at last come to him that what to Peter and to himself had seemed a most fascinating game was to others a struggle, grim and momentous. He recognized that until now General Rojas had never been to him a flesh-and-blood person, that he had not appreciated that his rescue meant actual life and happiness. He had considered him rather as one of the pieces in a game of chess, which Peter and himself were secretly playing against the Commandant of the San Carlos prison. And now, here, confronting him, was a human being, living, breathing, suffering, the daughter of this chessman, bone of his bone, flesh of his flesh, demanding of the stranger by what right he made himself her father's champion, by what right he pushed himself into the tragedy of the Rojas family. In his embarrassment Roddy

THE WHITE MICE

decided desperately to begin at the very beginning, to tell the exact truth, to omit nothing, and then to throw himself upon the mercy of the court.

The gray mist of the morning had lifted. Under the first warm rays of the sun, like objects developing on a photographer's plate, the cactus points stood out sharp and clear, the branches of the orange trees separated, assuming form and outline, the clusters of fruit took on a faint touch of yellow. From the palace yard in distant Willemstad there drifted toward them the boom of the morning gun.

With his reins over his arm, his sombrero crumpled in his hands, his face lifted to the face of the girl, Roddy stood in the road at attention, like a trooper reporting to his superior officer.

"We were in the tea-house of the Hundred and One Steps," said Roddy. "We called ourselves the White Mice."

Speaking quickly he brought his story down to the present moment. When he had finished, Inez, who had been bending toward him, straightened herself in the saddle and sat rigidly erect. Her lips and brows were drawn into two level lines, her voice came to him from an immeasurable distance.

"Then it was a joke?" she said.

"A joke!" cried Roddy hotly. "That's most unfair. If you will only give us permission we'll prove to you that it is no joke. Perhaps, as I told it, it sounded heartless. I told it badly. What could I say—that I am sorry? Could I, a stranger, offer sympathy to you? But we *are* sorry. Ever since Peter proposed it, ever since I saw your father——"

The girl threw herself forward, trembling. Her eyes opened wide.

"You saw my father!" she exclaimed. "Tell me," she begged, "did he look well? Did he speak to you? When did you—" she stopped suddenly, and turning her face from him, held her arm across her eyes.

"It was four months ago," said Roddy. "I was not allowed to speak to him. We bowed to each other. That was all."

"I must tell them," cried the girl, "they must know that I have seen some one who has seen him. But if they know I have seen you——"

She paused; as though asking advice she looked questioningly at Roddy. He shook his head.

"I don't understand," he said.

"My mother and sister don't know that I am here," Inez told him. "If they did they would be very angry. No one," she added warningly, "must know. They are afraid of you. They cannot understand why you offer to help us. And they mistrust you. That is why I had to see you here in this way." With a shrug of distaste the girl glanced about her. "Fortunately," she added, "you understand."

"Why, yes," Roddy assented doubtfully. "I understand your doing what *you* did, but I don't understand the others. Who is it," he asked, "who mistrusts me? Who," he added smiling, "besides yourself?"

"My mother," answered Inez directly, "your consul, Captain Codman, Colonel Vega, and ———"

In surprise, Roddy laughed and raised his eyebrows.

"Vega!" he exclaimed. "Why should Vega mistrust me?" Knowing what was in his mind, the girl made him a formal little bow.

"It is not," she answered, "because you saved his life." In obvious embarrassment she added: "It is because you are not in the confidence of your father. You can see that that must make it difficult for Colonel Vega."

Bewildered, Roddy stared at her and again laughed.

"And what possible interest," he demanded, "can *my* father have in Colonel Vega?"

For a moment, with distrust written clearly

in her eyes, the girl regarded him reproachfully. Then she asked coldly:

"Do you seriously wish me to think that you do *not* know that?"

While they had been speaking, even when Inez had made it most evident to Roddy that to herself and to her friends he was a discredited person, he had smiled patiently. His good humor had appeared unassailable. But now his eyes snapped indignantly. He pressed his lips together and made Inez an abrupt bow.

"I assure you, I know nothing," he said quickly.

He threw the reins over the neck of the pony, and with a slap on its flank drove it across the road within reach of the waiting Pedro. Then lifting his hat, and with another bow, he started in the direction of Willemstad. Inez, too surprised to speak, sat staring after him. But before he had taken a dozen steps, as though she had called him back and asked him to explain, he halted and returned. He had entirely recovered his good humor, but his manner when he spoke was not conciliatory.

"The trouble is this," he said, "your friends are so deep in plots that they have lost sight of the thing that counts. While they are 'mistrusting,' and suspecting, and spying on each other, a man is dying. I know that much, anyway. That is all I care to know." As though it were an extenuating fact, he added: "It is a question of character. It is a Venezuelan way of doing things. But it is not our way. It was very kind of you to give me this chance to explain our interfering. But I see now—everybody," he added dryly, "has taken pains to make it very plain—that we are a nuisance." He paused, and to assure her it was not she he was upbraiding, smiled cheerfully. In his most confidential manner he continued lightly: "For myself, I have always thought there was something to say for the fools who rush in where angels fear to tread. I remember once seeing a fool rush into a burning building and rescue a child, while I and some other angels shouted for ladders." He nodded, and again lifted his hat. "Good-by," he said, "and thank you." Leaving her seated silent in the saddle, he walked away.

This time he had turned the bend in the road and had proceeded along it some hundred yards, when from behind him he heard approaching at a reckless pace the hoof-beats of a pony. Looking back, he saw a whirlwind of fluttering skirts and scattered sparks and pebbles. Inez, followed by Pedro, drew up even with him; and as she dragged her pony to a halt, threw herself free of the pommel and dropped at his feet to the road. Had he not caught her by the shoulders she would have stumbled into his arms. A strand of hair had fallen across her face, her eyes were eager, flashing. She raised her gloved hands impulsively, and clasped them before him.

"Please!" she begged. "You must not go. It is true—what you say about us, but you must help us. I did not know. I had forgotten. It is three years since I talked to any one—any one from your country. I had forgotten. It is true; we are suspicious, we are *not* straightforward like you, like the people in the States. But you must not punish us for that. Not *me!*"

At all times the face raised to his was beautiful. Now, the delicate lips, like those of a child before it breaks into sobs, were trembling, the eyes, lifted appealingly, were eloquent with tears.

"You must advise me," said the girl. "You must help me."

She raised her clasped hands higher. She regarded him wistfully. "Won't you?" she begged.

Her attack had been swift, masterly; every feminine weapon had been brought into effective action; and the surrender of Roddy was

THE WHITE MICE

sudden, and complete. In abject submission he proceeded incoherently:

"My dear young lady!" he cried. "But, my dear young *lady!*"

He was rewarded with a brilliant, blinding smile.

"Then you *will* help me?" Inez asked.

Roddy recovered himself quickly.

"My Spanish is very bad," he answered, "but what it sounds like in English is, 'I am at your feet.'"

The sun now was shining brightly, and in the open road they were as conspicuous as though they had stood in a shop window on Broadway. Across the road, in the hedge opposite, a gate barred a path that led into one of the plantations. Roddy opened the gate, and together, followed by Pedro with the ponies, they found a spot where they were hidden by the hedge from any one passing on the highway. Inez halted in the shade of one of the orange trees. Speaking rapidly, she sketched for Roddy a brief history of the various efforts that had been made to rescue her father. She explained why these efforts had failed. She told him of the revolution led by Pino Vega, and the good it was expected to accomplish.

At first the girl spoke in some embarrassment. She knew that to be where she was, at that hour, alone with a stranger, was, in the eyes of her friends and family, an unpardonable offense. And though she resented their point of view, the fact that it existed disquieted her. But the man at her side did not seem to consider talking to a girl in the open sunshine either as a novel experience or one especially disgraceful. Politely, with lowered eyes, he gave to what she said the closest attention. The circumstance that they were alone, even the fact that she was young and attractive, did not once appear to occur to him. Seeing this, Inez with each succeeding moment gained confidence in Roddy and in herself and spoke freely.

"That is what we have tried to do," she said. "Now I am going to tell you why I asked you to meet me here this morning, and how I believe you can help me. Three days ago I received a message from my father."

Roddy exclaimed with interest, but motioned eagerly for her to continue.

"It is in cipher," she continued, "but it is his handwriting. It is unmistakable. It was given to me when I was at church. I was kneeling in the chapel of St. Agnes, which is in the darkest corner of the building. At first I was alone, and then a woman came and knelt close beside me. She was a negress, poorly dressed, and her face was hidden by her shawl. For a moment I thought she was murmuring her prayers, and then I found she was repeating certain words and that she was talking at me. 'I have a letter, a letter from your father,' she whispered. I crowded closer, and she dropped a piece of paper in front of me and then got to her feet and hurried away. I followed, but there were many people at mass, and when I had reached the street she had disappeared. The message she brought me is this: 'Page 54, paragraph 4.' That is all. It is the second message we have had from my father in two years. The first one was by word of mouth, and came a month ago. The meaning of that was only too plain. But what this one means I cannot imagine, nor," proceeded Inez with distress, "can I see why, if he had the chance to write to us, he did not write more openly."

She looked appealingly at Roddy, and paused for him to speak.

"He was afraid the message would be intercepted," said Roddy. "What he probably means to do is to send it to you in two parts. The second message will be the key that explains this one. He knew if he wrote plainly, and it fell into the wrong hands—" Roddy interrupted himself, and for a moment remained silent. "'Page 54, paragraph 4,'" he repeated. "Has he sent you a book?" he asked. "Has any book come to you anonymously?"

The girl shook her head. "No, I thought of that," she said, "but no books have come to us that we haven't ordered ourselves."

"What do the others think?" asked Roddy.

The girl colored slightly and shook her head. "I have not told them. I knew my mother would ask Pino to help her, and," she explained, "though I like Pino, for certain reasons I do not wish to be indebted to him for the life of my father. Before appealing to him I have been trying for two days to find out the meaning of the cipher, but I could not do it, and I was just about to show it to my mother when Captain Codman told us of your offer. That made me hesitate. And then, as between you and Pino, I decided you were better able to help us. You live in Porto Cabello, within sight of the prison. Pino will be in the field. His revolution may last a month, it may last for years. During that time he would do nothing to help my father. When you risked being shot yesterday, it seemed to me you showed you had spirit, and also, *you* are from the States, and Pino is a Venezuelan, so——"

"You needn't take up the time of the court," said Roddy, "in persuading me that I am the man to help you. To save time I will concede that. What was the other message you received from your father?"

The eyes of the girl grew troubled and her voice lost its eagerness.

"It was charged in a French paper," she said, "that the prisoners in San Carlos were being killed by neglect. The French minister is a friend of our family, and he asked Alvarez to appoint a committee of doctors to make an investigation. Alvarez was afraid to refuse, and sent the doctors to examine my father and report on his health. One of them told him that Alvarez would permit him to send a message to my mother, and to tell her himself whether he was, or was not, ill. This is the message that they gave us as coming from my father.

"'I don't know what you gentlemen may decide as to my health,' he said, 'but *I* know that I am dying. Tell my wife that I wish to be buried in my native country, and to place upon my tombstone my name and this epitaph: "He wrote history, and made history."'"
The voice of the girl had dropped to a whisper. She recovered herself and continued sadly: "Until three days ago that is the only word we have received from my father in two years."

The expression on Roddy's face was one of polite incredulity. Seeing this, Inez, as though answering his thought, said proudly: "My father made history when he arranged the boundary line between British Guiana and Venezuela."

Roddy shook his head impatiently.

"I wasn't thinking of that," he said. "I was thinking of the message. It doesn't sound a bit like your father," he exclaimed. "Not like what *I've* heard of him."

The eyes of the girl grew anxious with disappointment.

"Do you mean," she asked, "that you think he did *not* send that message?"

"It doesn't sound to me," said Roddy, "like the sort of message he would send, knowing the pain it would cause. He isn't the sort of man to give up hope, either. Even if it were true, why should he tell your mother he is dying? And that epitaph!" cried Roddy excitedly. "*That's* not like him, either! It is not modest." With sudden eagerness he leaned toward her. "*Did* your father write history?" he demanded.

Unable to see the purpose of his question, the girl gazed at him in bewilderment. "Why, of course," she answered.

"And does any part of it refer to Porto Cabello?"

After a moment of consideration Inez nodded.

THE WHITE MICE

"The third chapter," she said, "tells of the invasion by Sir Francis Drake."

"'Chapter three, page fifty-four, paragraph four!'" shouted Roddy. "I'll bet my head on it! Don't you see what he has done?" he cried. "He sent you the key before he sent you the cipher. The verbal message is the key to the written one. They gave him a chance to send word to your mother, and he took it. He told her he was dying only that he might give her a direction, apparently about an epitaph, a boastful epitaph. He never boasted while he was alive—why should he boast on his tombstone? His real message is this: 'Look in the history I wrote of Venezuela, on page fifty-four, paragraph four,' and when we have found it," cried Roddy, "we'll have found the way to get him out of prison!"

Inez was not convinced, but his enthusiasm was most inspiring.

"We have the history at the house," she cried, "and I know you can find it in the Spanish bookstore in Willemstad. I must go at once."

She moved forward, greatly excited, her eyes lit with the happiness of this new hope. Roddy ran to bring her pony, and making a bridge of his hands lifted her to the saddle. "If I am right about this," he said, "I must see you again to-day. Where can I meet you?"

In spite of her eagerness, the girl hesitated. One by one the traditions of a lifetime were smashing about her.

"I *must* tell my mother," she pleaded. "And I know she will not allow me——"

"And she'll tell Pino," interrupted Roddy. To detain her, he laid his hand upon the reins and shook them sharply.

"Are you helping Pino to win a revolution," he demanded, "or are you helping me to get your father out of prison?"

Inez gazed at him in dismay. In her brief twenty-two years no man had spoken to her in such a manner. Among her friends she knew of no Venezuelan who, no matter what the provocation, would have addressed his wife, his sister, his daughter in a tone so discourteous. And yet this stranger was treating her, who, as she had been frequently and reliably informed, was the loveliest and most lovable of her sex, as he might a mutinous younger brother. In spite of the new and serious thought that now occupied her mind, this one was also sufficiently novel to compel her attention. It both amused and fascinated her. Here was at last one man who was working to help her father, and not only in order to find favor in her bright eyes.

He needed her wits and her courage; he wanted her help, but he wanted it as from a comrade, as he would have asked it of another man. Unconsciously he was paying her the compliment that best pleased her. When she nodded in assent she laughed delightedly, partly at him for bullying, partly at herself that she should for a moment have resented it.

"I am helping *you!*" she said.

Not understanding why she laughed, Roddy regarded her doubtfully.

Imitating the directness of his manner, Inez spoke quickly. "You can keep the pony. It is new to our stable and not known to belong to us. To-morrow morning, before sunrise, ride out again, but this time take the road to Otrabanda and along the cliff. Be sure to pass our house before sunrise. Ride about a mile and turn down a bridle-path to your left. That will bring you to the beach. If I cannot go, Pedro will meet you. You will get the history my father wrote at Belancourts, in Willemstad." For a moment she regarded him with friendly eyes. "If you should be right," she exclaimed, "how can I ever thank you?"

Roddy smiled back at her and shook his head.

"I don't know that we were exactly looking for gratitude," he said. "Now, go!" he ordered, "for I can't leave until you are well out of sight."

With another delightful laugh, that to Roddy was again inexplicable, the girl accepted her dismissal. It was her first rendezvous, but, in spite of her inexperience, she knew that had it been made with a Venezuelan the man would not have been the one first to bring it to an end.

Roddy impatiently waited until a quarter of an hour had passed, then galloped to Willemstad. On the way he put up the pony at a livery-stable in the suburbs, and on foot made his way as quickly as possible to the bookstore. What he wanted, he explained, were guide-books and histories of Venezuela. Among those the man showed him was one in three volumes, in Spanish, by Señor Don Miguel Rojas. Roddy's fingers itched to open it, but he restrained himself and, after buying half a dozen other books, returned to his hotel. Peter was still asleep, and he could not wait to waken him. Locking himself in, he threw the books he did not want upon the floor, and, with fingers that were all thumbs, fumbled at the first volume of the history until he had found page fifty-four. His eyes ran down it to the fourth paragraph. His knowledge of Spanish was slight, but it was sufficient. Page fifty-four was the description of an attack from the sea by Drake, upon the Fortress of San Carlos. Translated by Roddy, paragraph four read as follows: "Seeing that it was no longer possible to hold the fortress, the defenders were assembled in the guard-room, and from there conducted to the mainland, through the tunnel that connects San Carlos with the Fortress of El Morro."

Like a man in a trance, Roddy walked to the adjoining room and shook the sleeping Peter by the shoulder. Peter opened his eyes, and the look in Roddy's face startled him into instant wakefulness.

"What's wrong?" he demanded.

"Nothing!" said Roddy. Forgetting that to Peter it was unintelligible, he pointed with a triumphant finger at paragraph four.

"I have found an underground passage into the cell of General Rojas," he said. "We must go back and dig him out."

In order to avoid the heat, those planters who lived some distance from Willemstad were in the habit of rising by candlelight, and when the sun rose it found them well advanced upon their journey. So when on the following morning Roddy again set forth to meet Inez Rojas, the few servants who knew of his early departure accepted it, and the excuse he gave of wild-pigeon shooting, as a matter of course.

Without difficulty Roddy found the bridle-path leading down from the cliff road to the sea, and after riding for a short distance along the beach came upon Inez, guarded by the faithful Pedro. The cliff, hollowed at its base by the sea, hung over them, hiding them from any one on the cliff road, and the waves, breaking into spray on an outer barrier of rock, shut them from the sight of those at sea.

As Inez rose from the rock on which she had been seated and came eagerly to meet him, her face was radiant with happiness. Over night she appeared to have gained in health and strength, to have grown younger, and, were it possible, more beautiful. The satisfaction in the eyes of Roddy assured her that he, also, had solved the riddle.

"You have seen the book," she called; "you understand?"

"I think so," replied Roddy. "Anyway, I've got a sort of blueprint idea of it. Enough," he added, "to work on."

"I didn't tell my mother," Inez announced. "Nor," she continued, as though defying her own misgivings, "do I mean to tell her. Until you can get back word to me, until you say that *this* time you believe we may hope, it seems to me it would be kinder to keep her in ignorance. But I told Pedro," she added.

THE WHITE MICE

She flashed a grateful smile at the old man, and he bowed and smiled eagerly in return. "And he has been able to help me greatly. He tells me," she went on, "that his father, who was in the artillery, was often stationed at Morro before it was abandoned. That was fifty years ago. The tunnel was then used daily and every one knew of it. But when the troops were withdrawn from Morro the passage was walled up and each end blocked with stone. In San Carlos it opened into the guard-room. El Morro was hardly a fortress. It was more of a signal-station. Originally, in the days of the pirates, it was used as a lookout. Only a few men were kept on guard there, and only by day. They slept and messed at San Carlos. Each morning they were assembled in the guard-room, and from there marched through the tunnel to El Morro, returning again at sunset."

"I don't know El Morro," said Roddy.

"You have probably seen it," Inez explained, "without knowing it was a fort. It's in ruins now. Have you noticed," she asked, "to the right of the town, a little hill that overlooks the harbor? It is just above the plain where the cattle are corralled until they are shipped to Cuba. Well, the ruins of El Morro are on top of that hill. It is about a quarter of a mile from San Carlos, so we know that is the length of the tunnel. Pedro tells me, for a part of the way it runs under the water of the harbor. It was cut through the solid rock by the prisoners at San Carlos."

"There must be a lot of people," objected Roddy, "who know of it."

"Fifty years ago they knew of it," returned Inez eagerly, "but, remember, for half a century it has virtually ceased to exist. And besides, to my people there is nothing unusual in such a tunnel. You will find them connected with every fort the Spaniards built along this coast, and in Cuba, and on the Isthmus of Panama. All along the Spanish Main, wherever there is more than one fort, you will find them linked together by tunnels. They were intended to protect the soldiers from the fire of the enemy while they were passing from one position to another."

The young people had been standing ankle-deep in the soft, moist sand. Now the girl moved toward her pony, but Roddy still stood looking out to sea. He appeared to have entirely forgotten that Inez was present, and to be intently regarding the waves that surged against the rocks, and burst into glittering walls of foam. At last, with a serious countenance, he came toward her.

THE WHITE MICE

"I shall tell the authorities at Porto Cabello," he said, "that they ought to build a light-house on El Morro. At any rate, I will ask permission to make a survey. As they don't intend to pay father for any of his light-houses, they are not likely to object. And as I don't intend to build one, father can't object. He will attribute my offer to mistaken zeal on behalf of the company. And he will consider it another evidence of the fact that I don't understand his business. As soon as I find out anything definite I will let you know. And, by the way," he asked, "*how* am I to let you know?"

Inez gave him the address of a fellow-exile from Venezuela, living in Willemstad, who was in secret communication with Pedro. Through this man letters would reach her safely.

She turned to him in farewell, and held out her hand.

"You must be very careful," she said.

"Trust me!" answered Roddy heartily. "I promise you I'll be as mysterious a double-dealer as any Venezuelan that ever plotted a plot. I admit," he went on, "that when I came down here I was the frank, wide-eyed child, but, I assure you, I've reformed. Your people have made me a real Metternich, a genuine Machiavelli. Compared to me now, a Japanese business man is as honest and truth-loving as Mrs. Wiggs of the Cabbage Patch."

With a grin, Roddy invited the girl to sympathize with his effort to conceal the seriousness of their undertaking, but she regarded him doubtfully, and frowned. In his heart Roddy felt sorry for her. It hurt him to think that any one so charming could not accept his theory, that the only way to treat a serious matter was with flippancy. But the girl undeceived him.

"You don't understand me," she said quietly. "I didn't mean to be careful to protect our interests. I meant you to be careful of yourself. If anything were to happen to you through this—" She hesitated and looked away from him toward the sea. "Do you imagine," she demanded, "that it is easy for me to ask what I am asking of you? *I* know I have no right to do it. I know the only possible excuse for me is that I am not asking it for myself, but for my father—although, of course, that *is* asking it for myself."

"Beauty in distress," began Roddy briskly, "is the one thing——"

"That's what I mean," interrupted the girl gratefully, "the way you take it, the way you make it easier for me. Every other man I know down here would tell me he was doing it only for me, and he would hope I would believe him. But when *you* say you are helping beauty in distress, you are secretly frightened lest I may not have a sense of humor—and believe you. I know you are doing this because you feel deeply for my father. If I didn't know that, if I didn't feel that that were true, all this I have asked of you would be impossible. But it is possible, because I know you first tried to save my father of your own accord. Because I know now that it is your nature to wish to help others. Because you are brave, and you are generous."

But Roddy refused to be ennobled.

"It's because I'm a White Mice," he said. "My oath compels me! How would you like," he demanded, frowning, "if we turned you into an Honorary White Mouse?"

For an instant, with perplexed eyes and levelled brows, the girl regarded him fixedly. Then she smiled upon him. It was the same flashing, blinding smile which the morning before had betrayed him into her hands, bound and captive. It was a smile that passed swiftly, like a flash of sunshine over a garden of gay flowers. It brought out unsuspected, ambushed dimples. It did fascinating and wholly indefensible things to her lips. It filled her eyes with gracious, beautiful meanings. Inez raised her head challengingly.

"You think," she declared, "that I cannot be foolish, too. But I can. Let's sit down here on this rock and be quite foolish."

V

"I can be quite as foolish as you," Inez repeated as Roddy continued to regard her. "Some day, when this is over, when you have made it all come right, we will sit out here and pretend that we have escaped from Venezuela, that we are up North in my mother's country— in your country. We will play these are the rocks at York Harbor, and we'll be quite young and quite happy. Have you ever sat on the rocks at York Harbor," she demanded eagerly, "when the spray splashed you, and the waves tried to catch your feet?"

Roddy was regarding her in open suspicion. He retreated warily.

"York Harbor!" he murmured. "I discovered it! It is named after me. But you! I never imagined you'd been there, and I never imagined you could be anything but serious, either. It makes you quite dangerous."

"Dangerous?" murmured the girl.

"One is dangerous," said Roddy, "when one is completely charming."

The girl frowned, and her shoulders moved slightly. "You speak," she said, "like a Venezuelan."

THE WHITE MICE

But Roddy was in no mood to accept reproof.

"I told you," he said, "I admire the fools who rush in where angels fear to tread. There is another man I admire equally, 'the man who runs away.' It takes great courage to run away. I must do it now."

He retreated from her. His eyes were filled with a sudden, deep delight in her, and a growing wonder. The girl regarded him steadily.

"Come here," she commanded, "and say 'Good-by' to me."

Roddy took the slim, gauntleted hand stretched out to him, and for an instant the girl held his hand firmly, and then nodded. The smile this time was very near to tears.

"What you are going to do," she said, "is the dangerous thing. You don't know how dangerous. If I should not see you again——"

Roddy looked down into her eyes, and laughed from utter happiness.

"You will see *me* again," he said.

His tone gave to the words a meaning which the girl entirely disregarded.

"You will remember," she went on, as though he had not spoken, "that we—that I am grateful."

Roddy turned and smiled out at the sunlit sea.

"You have given me," he answered, "other things to remember."

THE WHITE MICE

He pulled off his sombrero and took the gauntleted hand in both of his. He bowed over it and brushed it with his lips. The girl still regarded him steadily, questioningly.

"Good-by," faltered Roddy.

His eyes sought hers wistfully, appealingly, with all that he felt showing in them. But her own told him nothing. Roddy released her hand with an effort, as though it were bound to his with manacles.

"Now I know," he said gently, "why I came to Venezuela."

The girl made no answer, and silently Roddy mounted and rode away. When he had reached the place where the rocks would hide her from sight he glanced back. He saw Inez standing beside her pony, leaning with her arms across the saddle, looking after him. Then, as he waved his hand, she raised hers with a gesture that seemed to Roddy partly a farewell, partly a benediction.

The stable at which Roddy had told Pedro he would leave the pony was far in the suburbs, and by the time he had walked to Willemstad the morning was well advanced.

As he approached the quay he recognized that in his absence some event of unusual interest had claimed the attention of the people. Everywhere men were gathered in little groups, gesticulating, laughing, frowning importantly, and at the hotel Roddy was surprised to see, on the balcony leading from his room, Peter and the American Consul. The sight of him apparently afforded them great satisfaction, and they waved and beckoned to him frantically. Ignoring their last meeting, the Consul greeted Roddy as though he were an old friend.

"Have you heard the news?" he demanded. "It is of great local interest, and it should interest you. Last night," he explained, "President Alvarez declared an amnesty for his political opponents living in foreign countries. All exiles may now return to their homes."

He pointed at the small passenger steamer lying at the quay directly below the window. The *Blue Peter* was at the fore, and her deck was crowded with excited, jubilant Venezuelans.

"You see," explained Captain Codman, "they have lost no time."

In a tone that precluded the possibility of discussion, Peter briskly added: "And *we* are going with them. I have packed your bag and paid the bill. We sail in an hour."

The news of the amnesty bewildered Roddy. The wonderful possibilities it so suddenly presented thrilled him. They were so important that with difficulty he made his voice appear only politely interested.

"Now I know . . . why I came to Venezuela."

"And Señora Rojas?" he asked.

"I regret to say," answered Captain Codman, "she decides to take advantage of the amnesty. As soon as she can arrange her affairs here she will return to Miramar, her home in Porto Cabello."

To Miramar! Roddy turned suddenly to the window, and with unseeing eyes stared at the busy harbor. By sight he knew the former home of the Rojas family. In his walks he had often passed before its yellow-pillared front and windows barred with intricate screens of wrought iron. Through the great gates that had hung before Miramar since it had been the palace of the Spanish Governor-General, and through which four horses could pass abreast, he had peered at the beautiful gardens. He had wondered at the moss-covered statues, at the orchids on the flamboyant trees, with their flowers of scarlet, at the rare plants, now neglected and trailing riotously across the paths, choked with unkempt weeds. Not an hour before, when he had parted from Inez, he had determined to make sentimental journeys to that same house. For she had walked in those gardens, it was through those gates she had swept in her carriage to take the air in the Plaza; at night, when she slept, some high-ceilinged, iron-barred room of that house had sheltered her. He had pictured himself prowling outside the empty mansion and uncared-for garden, thinking of the exile, keeping vigil in the shadow of her home, freshly resolving to win back her father to health and freedom.

And now, by a scratch of the pen, the best that could happen had come to him. The house would waken to life. Instead of only the fragrance clinging to the vase, the rose itself would bloom again. Again Inez would walk under the arch of royal palms, would drive in the Alameda, would kneel at mass in the cool, dark church, while, hidden in the shadows, he could stand and watch her. And though, if he hoped to save her father, stealth and subterfuge would still be necessary, he could see her, perhaps, speak to her; at least by the faithful Pedro he could send her written words, flowers, foolish gifts, that were worth only the meaning they carried with them.

Feeling very much of a hypocrite, Roddy exclaimed fervently:

"How wonderful for Señora Rojas. To be near him again! Is she happy? Does it make it easier for her?"

With a disturbed countenance the Consul nodded gravely.

"Yes," he answered, "she welcomed the change. She believes it means for her husband better conditions. She hopes even for his pardon; but—" The Consul shook his head impatiently, and with pitying eyes looked down upon the excited men on the steamer below them.

"But what?" demanded Roddy.

"I suspect every act of Alvarez," the Consul explained. "This *looks* like the act of a generous opponent. But I cannot believe it is that. I believe he knows all that is being plotted against him. I believe this act of amnesty is only a device to put the plotters where he can get his hand on them. He is the spider inviting the flies into his parlor."

As the little steamer passed the harbor mouth and pushed her nose toward Porto Cabello, Roddy, with Peter at his side, leaned upon the starboard rail. Roddy had assured Inez that Peter must be given their full confidence, and he now only waited a fitting moment to tell him of what had occurred that morning, in so far, at least, as it referred to the tunnel.

The eyes of both were turned toward Casa Blanca, now rapidly retreating from them. And, as they watched it, the mind of each occupied with thoughts of its inmates, they saw a white figure leave the house, and, moving slowly, halt at the edge of the cliff.

Roddy, his eyes straining toward the coast-line, took off his hat and stood with it clasped in his hands. Peter saw the movement, and to hide a smile of sympathy, looked down at the white foam rushing below them.

"Roddy," he asked, "what sort of a girl is Inez Rojas?"

His eyes still seeking the figure on the rocks, and without turning his head, Roddy answered with startling directness:

"What sort of a girl?" he growled. "The sort of a girl *I* am going to marry!"

More moved than he knew, and thinking himself secure in the excited babel about him and in the fact that the others spoke in Spanish, Roddy had raised his voice. He was not conscious he had done so until, as he spoke, he saw a man leaning on the rail with his back toward him, give an involuntary start. Furious with himself, Roddy bit his lip, and with impatience waited for the man to disclose himself. For a moment the stranger remained motionless, and then, obviously to find out who had spoken, slowly turned his head. Roddy found himself looking into the glowing, angry eyes of Pino Vega. Of the two men, Roddy was the first to recover. With eagerness he greeted the Venezuelan; with enthusiasm he expressed his pleasure at finding him among his fellow-passengers, he rejoiced that Colonel Vega no longer was an exile. The Venezuelan, who had approached trembling with resentment, sulkily murmured his thanks. With a hope that sounded more like a threat that they would soon meet again, he begged to be allowed to rejoin his friends.

"Now you've done it!" whispered Peter cheerily. "And he won't let it rest there, either."

"Don't you suppose I know that better than you do," returned Roddy miserably. He beat the rail with his fist. "It should not have happened in a thousand years," he wailed. "He must not know I have ever even seen her."

"He *does* know," objected Peter, coming briskly to the point. "What are you going to do?"

"Lie to him," said Roddy. "He is an old friend of the family. She told me so herself. She thought even of appealing to him before she appealed to us. If he finds out I have met her alone at daybreak, I have either got to tell him why we met and what we are trying to do, or he'll believe, in his nasty, suspicious, Spanish-American way, that I am in love with her, and that she came there to let me tell her so."

Roddy turned on Peter savagely.

"*Why* didn't you stop me?" he cried.

"Stop *you*—talking too much?" gasped Peter. "Is that my position? If it is, I resign."

The moon that night threw black shadows of shrouds and ratlines across a deck that was washed by its radiance as white as a breadboard. In the social hall, the happy exiles were rejoicing noisily, but Roddy stood apart, far forward, looking over the ship's side and considering bitterly the mistake of the morning. His melancholy self-upbraidings were interrupted by a light, alert step, and Pino Vega, now at ease, gracious and on guard, stood bowing before him.

"I do not intrude?" he asked.

Roddy, at once equally on guard, bade him welcome.

"I have sought you out," said the Venezuelan pleasantly, "because I would desire a little talk with you. I believe we have friends in common."

"It is possible," said Roddy. "I have been in Porto Cabello about four months now."

"It was not of Porto Cabello that I spoke," continued Vega, "but of Curaçao." He looked into Roddy's eyes suddenly and warily, as a swordsman holds the eyes of his opponent. "I did not understand," he said, "that you knew the Rojas family?"

"I do not know them," answered Roddy.

Vega turned his back to the moon, so that his face was in shadow. With an impatient gesture he flicked his cigarette into the sea. As though he found Roddy's answer unsatisfactory, he paused. He appeared to wish that Roddy should have a chance to reconsider it. As the American remained silent, Vega continued, but his tone now was openly hostile.

"I have been Chief of Staff to General Rojas for years," he said. "I have the honor to know his family well. Señora Rojas treats me as she did her son, who was my dearest friend. I tell you this to explain why I speak of a matter which you may think does not concern me. This morning, entirely against my will, I overheard you speaking to your friend. He asked you of a certain lady. You answered boldly you intended to marry her." Vega's voice shook slightly, and he paused to control it. "Now, you inform me that you are not acquainted with the Rojas family. What am I to believe?"

"I am glad you spoke of that," said Roddy heartily. "I saw that you overheard us, and I was afraid you'd misunderstand me——"

The Venezuelan interrupted sharply.

"I am well acquainted with your language!"

"You speak it perfectly," Roddy returned, "but you did not understand it as I spoke it. The young lady is well known in Willemstad.

THE WHITE MICE

Our Consul, as you are aware, is her friend. He admires her greatly. He told me that she is half American. She has been educated like an American girl, she rides, she plays tennis. What my friend said to me was, 'What sort of a girl is Señorita Rojas?' and I answered, 'She is the sort of girl I am going to marry,' meaning she is like the girls in my own country, one of our own people, like one of the women I some day hope to marry."

Roddy smiled and shrugged his shoulders.

"Now do you understand?" he asked.

The Venezuelan gave no answering smile. His eyes shone with suspicion. Roddy recognized that between his desire to believe and some fact that kept him from believing, the man was acutely suffering.

"Tell me, in a word," demanded Vega sharply, "give me your word you do not know her."

"I don't see," said Roddy, "that this is any of your damned business!"

The face of Vega checked him. At his refusal to answer, Roddy saw the look of jealousy that came into the man's eyes and the torment it brought with it. He felt a sudden pity for him, a certain respect as for a fellow-sufferer. He himself had met Inez Rojas but twice, but, as he had told her, he knew now why he had

THE WHITE MICE

come to Venezuela. This older man had known Inez for years, and to Roddy, arguing from his own state of mind regarding her, the fact was evidence enough that Vega must love her also. He began again, but now quietly, as he would argue with a child.

"I see no reason for making any mystery of it," he said. "I did meet Miss Rojas. But I can't say I know her. I met her when she was out riding with her groom. I thought she was an American. She needed some help, which I was able to give her. That is all."

Vega approached Roddy, leaning forward as though he were about to spring on him. His eyes were close to Roddy's face.

"And what was the nature of this help?" he demanded.

"You are impertinent," said Roddy.

"Answer me!" cried the Venezuelan. "I have the right. No one has a better right."

He flung up his right arm dramatically, and held it tense and trembling, as though it were poised to hurl a weapon.

"You were watched!" he cried hysterically. "I *know* that you met. And you tried to deceive me. Both of you. She will try, also——"

The moonlight disappeared before the eyes of Colonel Vega, and when again he opened them he was looking dizzily up at the swaying masts and yards. Roddy, with his hand at Vega's throat, was forcing his shoulders back against the rail. His free hand, rigid and heavy as a hammer, swung above the Venezuelan's face.

"Yesterday," panted Roddy, "I saved your life. If you insult that girl with your dirty, Latin mind, so help me—I will *take* it!"

He flung the man from him, but Vega, choking with pain and mortification, staggered forward.

"It is *you* who insult her," he shrieked. "It is I who protect her. Do you know *why?* Do you know what she is to me? She is my promised wife!"

For a moment the two men stood, swaying with the gentle roll of the ship, staring into each other's eyes. Above the sound of the wind in the cordage and the whisper of the water against the ship's side, Roddy could hear himself breathing in slow, heavy respirations. Not for an instant did he doubt that the man told the truth. Vega had spoken with a conviction that was only too genuine, and his statement, while it could not justify, seemed to explain his recent, sudden hostility. With a sharp effort, Roddy recovered himself. He saw that no matter how deeply the announcement might affect him, Vega must believe that to the American it was a matter of no possible consequence.

"You should have told me this at first," he said quietly. "I thought your questions were merely impertinent."

Roddy hesitated. The interview had become poignantly distasteful to him. He wished to get away; to be alone. He was conscious that a possibility had passed out of his life, the thought of which had been very dear to him. He wanted to think, to plan against this new condition. In discussing Inez with this man, in this way, he felt he was degrading her and his regard for her. But he felt also that for her immediate protection he must find out what Vega knew and what he suspected. With the purpose of goading him into making some disclosure, Roddy continued insolently:

"And I still think they are impertinent."

Roddy's indignation rose and got the upper hand. He cast caution aside.

"With us," he continued, "when a woman promises to marry a man—he does not spy on her."

"We spied on *you*," protested Vega. "We did not think it would lead us to——"

Roddy cut him off with a sharp cry of warning.

"Be careful!" he challenged.

"You met in the road——"

"So I told you," returned Roddy.

"You dismounted and talked with her."

Roddy laughed, and with a gesture of impatience motioned Vega to be silent.

"Is that all?" he demanded.

The Venezuelan saw the figure he presented. Back of him were hundreds of years of Spanish traditions, in his veins was the blood of generations of ancestors by nature suspicious, doubting, jealous. From their viewpoint he was within his rights; they applauded, they gave him countenance; but by the frank contempt of the young man before him his self-respect was being rudely handled. Not even to himself could he justify his attitude.

"In my country," he protested, "according to our customs, it was enough."

The answer satisfied and relieved Roddy. It told him all he wished to know. It was now evident that Vega's agent had seen only the first meeting, that he was not aware that Inez followed after Roddy, or that the next morning by the seashore they had again met. The American brought the interview to an abrupt finish.

"I refuse," said Roddy loftily, "to discuss this matter with you further. If the mother of Señorita Rojas wishes it, I shall be happy to answer any questions she may ask. I have done nothing that requires explanation or apology. I am responsible to no one. Goodnight."

"Wait!" commanded Vega. "You will find that here you cannot so easily avoid responsibilities. You have struck me. Well, we have other customs, which gentlemen——"

"I am entirely at your service," said Roddy. He made as magnificent a bow as though he himself had descended from a line of Spanish grandees. Vega's eyes lit with pleasure. He was now playing a part in which he felt assured he appeared to advantage. He almost was grateful to Roddy for permitting him to reestablish himself in his own esteem.

"My friends shall wait upon you," he said.

"Whenever you like," Roddy answered. He started up the deck and returned again to Vega. "Understand me," he whispered, "as long as I'm enjoying the hospitality of your country I accept the customs of your country. If you'd made such a proposition to me in New York I'd have laughed at you." Roddy came close to Vega and emphasized his words with a pointed finger. "And understand *this!* We have quarrelled over politics. You made an offensive remark about Alvarez; I defended him and struck you. You now demand satisfaction. That is what happened. And if you drag the name of any woman into this I won't give you satisfaction. I will give you a thrashing until you can't stand or see."

Roddy found Peter in the smoking-room, and beckoning him on deck, told him what he had done.

"You're a nice White Mouse!" cried Peter indignantly. "You're not supposed to go about killing people; you're supposed to save lives."

"No one is ever killed in a duel," said Roddy; "I'll fire in the air, and he will probably miss me. I certainly hope so. But there will be one good result. It will show Alvarez that I'm not a friend of Vega's, nor helping him in his revolution."

"You don't have to shoot a man to show you're not a friend of his," protested Peter.

They were interrupted by the hasty approach of Vega's chief advisers and nearest friends, General Pulido and Colonel Ramon.

"Pino seems in a hurry," said Roddy. "I had no idea he was so bloodthirsty."

"Colonel Vega," began Pulido abruptly, "has just informed us of the unfortunate incident. We have come to tell you that no duel can take place. It is monstrous. The life of Colonel Vega does not belong to him, it belongs to the Cause. We will not permit him to risk it needlessly. You, of all people, should see that. You must apologize."

The demand, and the peremptory tone in which it was delivered, caused the fighting blood of Roddy's Irish grandfathers to bubble in his veins.

"'Must' and 'apologize'!" protested Roddy, in icy tones. "Those are difficult words, gentlemen."

"Consider," cried Pulido, "what great events hang upon the life of Colonel Vega."

"My own life is extremely interesting to me," said Roddy. "But I have done nothing which needs apology."

Colonel Ramon now interrupted anxiously.

"You risked your life for Pino. Why now do you wish to take it? Think of his importance to Venezuela, of the happiness he will bring his country, and think what his loss would mean to your own father."

"My father!" exclaimed Roddy. "What has my father to do with this?"

The two Venezuelans looked at each other in bewilderment, and then back at Roddy sternly and suspiciously.

"Are you jesting?" demanded General Pulido.

"Never been more serious in my life," said Roddy.

The two officers searched his face eagerly.

"It is as Pino says," exclaimed Pulido, with sudden enlightenment. "He is telling the truth!"

"Of course I'm telling the truth!" cried Roddy fiercely. "Are you looking for a duel, too?"

"Tell him!" cried Pulido.

"But Mr. Forrester's orders!" protested Colonel Ramon.

"He is more dangerous," declared Pulido, "knowing nothing, than he would be if he understood."

He cast a rapid glance about him. With a scowl, his eyes finally rested upon Peter.

"I'll be within knockout distance if you want me," said that young man to Roddy, and moved to the rail opposite.

When he had gone, Pulido bent eagerly forward.

"Do you not know," he demanded, "what it is your father is doing in our country?"

Roddy burst forth impatiently, "No!" he protested. "And I seem to be the only man in the country who doesn't."

The two officers crowded close to him. In sepulchral tones, Pulido exclaimed dramatically. He spoke as though he were initiating Roddy into a secret order.

THE WHITE MICE

"Then understand," he whispered, "that your father supports Pino Vega with five million bolivars; that Vega, whose life you are seeking, is the man your father means to make President of Venezuela. Now do you understand?"

For a long time Roddy remained silent. Then he exclaimed in tones of extreme exasperation:

"I understand," he said, "that, if my father had given me his telephone number, he would have saved me a lot of trouble. No wonder everybody suspects me."

"And now," declared Pulido anxiously, "you are one of *us!*"

"I am nothing of the sort," snapped Roddy. "If my father does not wish to tell me his plans I can't take advantage of what I learn of them from strangers. I shall go on," he continued with suspicious meekness, "with the work father has sent me here to do. Who am I, that I should push myself into the politics of your great country?"

"And the duel?" demanded Pulido.

"I am sure," hastily interjected Colonel Ramon, "if Colonel Vega withdraws his offensive remark about President Alvarez, Mr. Forrester will withdraw his blow."

Roddy failed to see how a blow that had left

THE WHITE MICE

a raw spot on the chin of Pino Vega could by mutual agreement be made to vanish. But if to the minds of the Spanish-Americans such a miracle were possible, it seemed ungracious not to consent to it.

"If I understand you," asked Roddy, "Colonel Vega withdraws his offensive remark?"

The seconds of Pino Vega nodded vigorously.

"Then," continued Roddy, "as there was no offensive remark, there could have been no blow, and there can be no duel."

Roddy's summing up delighted the Venezuelans, and declaring that the honor of all was satisfied, they bowed themselves away.

Next morning at daybreak the fortress of San Carlos rose upon the horizon, and by ten o'clock Roddy was again at work, threatening a gang of Jamaica coolies. But no longer he swore at them with his former wholeheartedness. His mind was occupied with other things. Now, between him and his work, came thoughts of the tunnel that for half a century had lain hidden from the sight of man; and of Inez, elusive, beautiful, distracting, now galloping recklessly toward him down a sunlit road, now a motionless statue standing on a white cliff, with the waves of the Caribbean bending and bowing before her.

With the return of the exiles to Porto Ca-

THE WHITE MICE

bello, that picturesque seaport became a place of gay reunions, of banquets, of welcome and rejoicing. The cafés again sprang to life. The Alameda was crowded with loitering figures and smart carriages, whilst the vigilance and activity of the government secret police increased. Roddy found himself an object of universal interest. As the son of his father, and as one who had prevented the assassination of Pino Vega, the members of the government party suspected him. While the fact that in defense of Alvarez he had quarrelled with Vega puzzled them greatly.

"If I can't persuade them I am with the government," said Roddy, "I can at least keep them guessing."

A week passed before Peter and Roddy were able, without arousing suspicion, and without being followed, to visit El Morro. They approached it apparently by accident, at the end of a long walk through the suburbs, and so timed their progress that, just as the sun set, they reached the base of the hill on which the fortress stood. They found that on one side the hill sloped gently toward the city, and on the other toward the sea. The face toward the city, except for some venturesome goats grazing on its scant herbage, was bare and deserted. The side that sloped to the sea was closely overgrown with hardy mesquite bushes and wild laurel, which would effectually conceal any one approaching from that direction. What had been the fortress was now only a broken wall, a few feet in height. It was covered with moss, and hidden by naked bushes with bristling thorns. Inside the circumference of the wall was a broken pavement of flat stones. Between these, trailing vines had forced their way, their roots creeping like snakes over the stones and through their interstices, while giant, ill-smelling weeds had turned the once open court-yard into a maze. These weeds were sufficiently high to conceal any one who did not walk upright, and while Peter kept watch outside the walled ring, Roddy, on his hands and knees, forced his way painfully from stone to stone. After a quarter of an hour of this slow progress he came upon what once had been the mouth of the tunnel. It was an opening in the pavement corresponding to a trap in a roof, or to a hatch in the deck of a ship. The combings were of stone, and were still intact, as were also the upper stones of a flight of steps that led down to the tunnel. But below the level of the upper steps, blocking further descent, were two great slabs of stone. They were buried deep in a bed of cement, and riveted together and to the walls of the tunnel by bands of iron. Roddy signalled for Peter to join him, and in dismay they gazed at the formidable mass of rusty iron, cement and stone.

"We might as well try to break into the Rock of Gibraltar!" gasped Peter.

"Don't think of the difficulties," begged Roddy. "Think that on the other side of that barrier an old man is slowly dying. I admit it's going to be a tough job. It will take months. But whatever a man has put together, a man can pull to pieces."

"I also try to see the bright side of life," returned Peter coldly, "but I can't resist pointing out that the other end of your tunnel opens into a prison. Breaking into a bank I can understand, but breaking into a prison seems almost like looking for trouble."

The dinner that followed under the stars in their own court-yard did much to dispel Peter's misgivings, and by midnight, so assured was he of their final success, that he declared it now was time that General Rojas should share in their confidence.

"To a man placed as he is," he argued, "hope is everything; hope is health, life. He must know that his message has reached the outside. He must feel that some one is working toward him. He is the entombed miner, and, to keep heart in him, we must let him hear the picks of the rescuing party."

"Fine!" cried Roddy, "I am for that, too. I'll get my friend Vicenti, the prison doctor, to show you over the fortress to-morrow. And we'll try to think of some way to give Rojas warning."

They at once departed for the café of the *Dos Hermanos*, where the gay youth of Porto Cabello were wont to congregate, and where they found the doctor. During the evening he had been lucky at baccarat, and had been investing his winnings in sweet champagne. He was in a genial mood. He would be delighted to escort the friend of Señor Roddy over the fortress, or to any other of the historical places of interest for which Porto Cabello was celebrated.

"Where Alvarez punishes traitors," exclaimed Roddy in a loud tone, "is what we most desire to see. And," he added, scowling darkly through the smoke-laden café, "if we could see others who are still at liberty in the same place we would be better pleased."

The remark, although directed at no one in particular, caused a sensation, and led several of those who had been for two years in exile to hurriedly finish their chocolate ices and seek their homes.

THE WHITE MICE

After making an appointment for the morrow with Doctor Vicenti, and when they were safe in their own *patio*, Peter protested mildly.

"Your devotion to Alvarez," he said, "is too sudden. You overdo it. Besides, it's making an expert liar of you. Don't get the habit."

"As the son of the man who is trying to destroy Alvarez," declared Roddy, "my position is extremely delicate. And next week it will be more so. McKildrick got a cable to-day saying that Sam Caldwell is arriving here by the next boat. His starting for Porto Cabello the very moment Vega arrives here means trouble for Alvarez, and that the trouble is coming soon. For, wherever you find Sam Caldwell, there you will find plotting, bribery, and all uncleanliness. And if I'm to help Rojas out of prison I must have nothing to do with Sam. Alvarez recognizes no neutrals. The man who is not with him is against him. So I must be the friend of Alvarez and of his creatures. For public occasions, my hand must be against the F. C. C., against Vega, and especially against Sam Caldwell, because everybody knows he is the personal agent of my father. Vega's friends know that my father treats me as though he could not trust me. The Alvarez crowd must know that, too. Even as it is, they think my being down here is a sort of punishment. None of them has ever worked in his life, and the idea of a rich man's son sweating at a donkey-engine with a gang of Conch niggers, means to them only that my father and I have quarrelled. It will be my object hereafter to persuade them that that is so. If I have to act a bit, or lie a bit, what are a few lies against the freedom of such a man as Rojas? So, to-morrow, if you should be so lucky as to see Rojas, don't be a bit surprised if I should insult that unhappy gentleman grossly. If I do, within an hour the fact will be all over the cafés and the plazas, and with Alvarez it would be counted to me for righteousness. Much that I may have to do of the same sort will make the gentlemen of Vega's party consider me an ungrateful son, and very much of a blackguard. They may, in their turn, insult me, and want to fight more duels. But it's all in the game. To save that old man is my only object for living, my only interest. I don't care how many revolutions I tread on. I would sacrifice everybody and everything—for him."

After his long speech, Roddy drew a deep breath and glared at Peter as though inviting contradiction. But, instead of contradicting him, Peter smiled sceptically and moved to his bedroom, which opened upon the courtyard. At the door he turned.

"'And the woman,' he quoted, 'was very fair.'"

The next morning the two Americans met Doctor Vicenti in the guard-room of the fortress, and under his escort began a leisurely inspection of the prison. They themselves saw to it that it was leisurely, and by every device prolonged it. That their interest in the one prisoner they had come to see might not be suspected, they pretended a great curiosity in the doctor's patients and in all the other prisoners. After each visit to a cell they would invite Vicenti to give them the history of its inmate. They assured him these little biographies, as he related them, were of surpassing brilliancy and pathos. In consequence, Vicenti was so greatly flattered that, before they reached the cell of General Rojas, each succeeding narrative had steadily increased in length, and the young doctor had become communicative and loquacious.

When at last they had descended to the lowest tier of cells, Vicenti paused and pointed toward an iron-barred double door.

"In there," he whispered to Peter, "is our most distinguished political prisoner, General Rojas. There is no one Alvarez would so willingly see dead. And, if he keeps him here a month longer, Alvarez will have his wish."

"But they say the man is a traitor," protested Roddy.

The doctor shrugged his shoulders.

"In my country," he answered, "every man who is not for the government is a traitor."

He directed the turnkey who accompanied them to unlock the gate of the cell, and with a gesture invited the Americans to enter. As they did so, each dropped his right hand into his outside coat pocket. When it came forth again, concealed under each little finger was a tiny roll of rice-paper torn from a book of cigarette-wrappers. On each, in pencil, was written "54–4" and the word "Hope." The night previous Peter and Roddy had prepared the papers, on the chance that while one of them occupied the attention of the guide, the other could slip his message to Rojas. Roddy had insisted upon the use of rice-paper, because it could be swallowed without indigestion, and instead of the word "Hope," had preferred a free-hand drawing of an anchor, arguing that the anchor was the emblem of hope, and was more picturesque than the written word. To this Peter had objected that while they knew an anchor signified hope, Rojas might not, and as they were risking their lives to get a message to him, it was important he should understand it. They compromised on the numerals, which would show Rojas his own cipher messages had been received and understood, and the word "Hope" was added to put heart into him and strengthen his desire to cling to life.

But on entering the cell they saw at once that there would be no chance to deliver their message. General Rojas was seated at a table some ten feet from them, and the turnkey, who had submitted with ill grace to the Americans entering any of the cells, and who seemed especially to resent their presence in this one, at once placed himself aggressively on guard.

As he did so he commanded sharply: "The visitors will not speak to the prisoner."

"That is understood," Vicenti answered.

The Americans saw a room some forty by twenty feet in size, with walls, arched ceiling and floor entirely of stone. There were no windows, but it was well lighted by candles, and the lanterns carried by Vicenti and the turnkey threw a full light into each corner. They saw a cot, a table, a chair, a number of shelves loaded to the bending point with books and, at one end of the cell, an immense archway. This archway had been blocked with stone, roughly hewn and held together by ce-

THE WHITE MICE

ment. At the first glance, it was obvious that this was the other entrance to the tunnel. As he beheld its solid front, the heart of each of the young men sank in dismay.

General Rojas had risen, and stood shading his eyes from the unaccustomed light of the lanterns.

"I have taken the liberty of intruding upon you," Vicenti was saying, "because these two gentlemen are interested in the history of the fortress."

General Rojas bowed gravely, and with a deprecatory gesture, glanced at the turnkey, as though to explain why he did not address them.

"This part of the fortress," Vicenti began hurriedly, "is very old. It was built in the sixteenth century, and was, I think, originally the messroom. It is now used only for the most important political prisoners."

For an instant there was an awkward silence, and then Roddy broke it with a laugh, short and contemptuous.

"You mean traitors," he sneered.

General Rojas straightened as suddenly as though Roddy had struck him. The young doctor was no less moved. He turned on the American with an exclamation of indignation.

"You forget yourself, sir!" he said.

THE WHITE MICE

Though Peter had been warned that Roddy might try by insulting Rojas to make capital for himself, his insolence to a helpless old man was unpardonable. He felt his cheeks burn with mortification. The turnkey alone showed his pleasure, and grinned appreciatively. Roddy himself was entirely unashamed.

"I have no sympathy for such men!" he continued defiantly. "A murderer takes only human life; a traitor would take the life of his country. In the States," he cried hotly, "we make short work with traitors. We hang them!"

He wheeled furiously on Peter, as though Peter had contradicted him.

"I say we do," he exclaimed. "It's in the Constitution. It's the law. You've read it yourself. It's page fifty-four, paragraph four, of the Constitution of the United States. 'Punishment for Traitors.' Page fifty-four, paragraph four."

Apparently with sudden remorse at his impetuosity, he turned to the doctor.

"I beg your pardon," he exclaimed. "I *did* forget myself. But to me, men like that are intolerable."

Vicenti was not to be mollified.

"Then you had better avoid their presence," he said angrily.

THE WHITE MICE

With an impatient gesture he motioned the two Americans into the corridor, and in distress approached the prisoner.

"I apologize, sir," he said, "for having subjected you to such an incident."

But General Rojas made no answer. To his surprise, Vicenti found that the old man was suffering from the scene even more keenly than he had feared. Like one suddenly bereft of strength, General Rojas had sunk into his chair. His bloodless, delicate hands trembled upon the table. Great tears crept down his white, wrinkled face. In the two years through which the young doctor had watched his patient he had never before seen in his eyes the strange, mad light that now shone there. To the medical man, it meant only that the end was nearer than he had supposed. Shocked and grieved, the doctor made a movement to withdraw.

"I am deeply sorry," he murmured.

General Rojas raised his head. With an effort he drew over his face its customary, deathlike mask.

"It is nothing!" he exclaimed. "What is one more insult, what is one more degradation, when I know that my end is near!" He raised his voice; it was strangely vigorous, youthful, jubilant; it carried through the open bars to

THE WHITE MICE

the far end of the corridor. "What does anything matter," he cried, "when I know—that the end is near!" His head sunk upon the table. To hide his tears, the General buried his face in his hands.

Outside, in the darkness, Peter clutched Roddy by the hand, and for an instant crushed it in his own.

"Do you hear?" he whispered. "He is answering you."

"Yes," stammered Roddy. The excitement or the dampness of the prison had set him shivering, and with the back of his hand he wiped the cold moisture from his forehead. He laughed mirthlessly. "Yes," he answered, "he understood me. And now, we've *got* to make good!"

That afternoon when the carriages of the aristocracy of Porto Cabello were solemnly circling the Plaza, Roddy came upon McKildrick, seated on one of the stone benches, observing the parade of local wealth and fashion with eyes that missed nothing and told nothing. McKildrick was a fine type of the self-taught American. He possessed a thorough knowledge of his profession, executive skill, the gift of handling men, and the added glory of having "worked his way up." He was tall, lean, thin-lipped, between thirty and forty years of age.

During business hours he spoke only to give an order or to put a question. Out of working hours, in his manner to his assistants and workmen, he was genially democratic. He had, apparently, a dread of being alone, and was seldom seen without one of the younger engineers at his elbow. With them he was considered a cynic, the reason given for his cynicism being that "the Chief" had tried to "take a fall out of matrimony," and had come out of it a woman-hater. Officially he was Roddy's superior, but it never was possible for any one in the pay of the F. C. C. to forget that Roddy was the son of his father. Even McKildrick, in certain ways, acknowledged it. One way was, in their leisure moments, not to seek out Roddy, but to wait for the younger man to make advances. On this occasion, after for a brief moment contemplating McKildrick severely, Roddy, with an impatient exclamation, as though dismissing doubts and misgivings, sat down beside him.

"McKildrick," he began impetuously, "I want to ask you an impertinent question. It concerns your moral character."

McKildrick grinned appreciatively.

"We court investigation," he said.

"Under what pressure to the square inch," demanded Roddy, "would a secret confided to you be liable to burst its boiler?"

"I've never," returned the engineer, "had an accident of that kind."

"Good!" exclaimed Roddy. "Then suppose I said to you, 'McKildrick, I know where there's buried treasure, but I don't know how to get it out.' You *would* know. Now, if I led you to the buried treasure, would you, as an expert engineer, tell me how to dig it out, and then could you forget you'd given that advice and that you'd ever heard of the treasure?"

For a moment McKildrick considered this hypothetical case. Then he asked: "Which bank are you thinking of opening?"

Roddy rose abruptly.

"I'll show you," he exclaimed.

That Roddy was acting, in spite of secret misgivings, was so evident, that McKildrick good-naturedly demurred.

"Better not tell me anything," he protested, "that you'll be sorry for when you're sober."

Roddy shook his head, and, not until they had left the suburbs and the last fisherman's hut behind them and were on the open coast, did he again refer to the subject of their walk. Then he exclaimed suddenly: "And I forgot to mention that if father finds out you advised me you will probably lose your job."

McKildrick halted in his tracks.

"It's a pity," he agreed, "that you forgot to

mention that. As a rule, when I give expert advice I get a fat check for it."

"And what's more," continued Roddy, "if Alvarez finds it out you'll go to jail."

"Your piquant narrative interests me strangely," said McKildrick. "What else happens to me?"

"But, of course," explained Roddy reassuringly, "you'll tell them you didn't know what you were doing."

"How about *your* telling me what we are doing?" suggested the engineer.

"From this point," was Roddy's only reply, "you crawl on your hands and knees, or some one may see you."

The engineer bent his tall figure and, following in Roddy's trail, disappeared into the laurel bushes.

"Why shouldn't they see me?" he called.

"One looks so silly on his hands and knees," Roddy suggested.

For ten minutes, except for the rustle of the bushes, they pushed their way in silence, and then Roddy scrambled over the fallen wall of the fort, and pointed down at the entrance to the tunnel.

"The problem is," he said, "to remove these slabs from that staircase, and leave it in such shape that no one who is foolish enough to climb up here could see that they had been disturbed."

"Do you really think," demanded McKildrick, smiling sceptically, "that there *is* buried treasure under these stones?"

"Yes," answered Roddy anxiously, "a *kind* of buried treasure."

Cautiously McKildrick raised his head, and, as though to establish his bearings, surveyed the landscape. To the north he saw the city; to the east, a quarter of a mile away, the fortress, separated from the mainland by a stretch of water; and to the south, the wild mesquite bushes and laurel through which they had just come, stretching to the coast.

"Is this a serious proposition?" he asked.

"It's a matter of life and death," Roddy answered.

McKildrick seated himself on the flight of stone steps, and for some time, in silence, studied them critically. He drove the heel of his boot against the cement, and, with his eyes, tested the resistance of the rusty bars of iron.

"With a couple of men and crowbars, and a pinch of dynamite that wouldn't make a noise," he said at last, "I could open that in an hour."

"Could you put it back again?" asked Roddy.

There was a long pause.

"I guess," said McKildrick, "you'll have to let me in on the ground floor."

The sun had set and the air had turned cold and damp. Roddy seated himself beside his chief and pointed at the great slabs at their feet. His voice dropped to a whisper.

"It's like this," he began.

When, two hours later, they separated at the outskirts of the city, McKildrick had been initiated into the Brotherhood of the White Mice.

They had separated, agreeing that in the future the less they were seen together the better. But, in wishing to be alone, Roddy had another and more sentimental reason.

Each evening since his return from Curaçao he had made a pilgrimage to the deserted home of the Rojas family, and, as the garden of Miramar ran down to meet the shore of the harbor, as did the garden of his own house, he was able to make the nocturnal visits by rowboat, and without being observed. Sometimes he was satisfied simply to lie on his oars opposite the empty mansion, and think of the young girl who, so soon, was to waken it to life; and again he tied his boat to a public wharf a hundred yards down the shore, and with the aid of the hanging vines pulled himself to the top of the seawall, and dropped into the garden. To a young man very much interested in a young woman, of whom he knew so little that it was possible to endow her with every grace of mind and character, and whose personal charm was never to be forgotten, these melancholy visits afforded much satisfaction. Even to pass the house was a pleasing exercise; and, separating from McKildrick, he turned his steps to the Alameda, the broad avenue shaded by a double line of trees that followed the curve of the harbor, and upon which the gates of Miramar opened. As he approached the house he saw, with surprise and pleasure, that in the future his midnight prowlings were at an end. Miramar was occupied. Every window blazed with light. In this light servants were moving hurriedly, and in front of the gates the Alameda was blocked with carts loaded with trunks and boxes.

Excited by the sight, Roddy hid himself in the shadows of the trees, and, unobserved, stood impatiently waiting for a chance to learn if the exiles had indeed returned to their own. He had not long to wait. In a little figure bustling among the carts, and giving many orders, he recognized his friend and ally, Pedro. Roddy instantly stepped into the glare of the electric globes until he was sure Pedro had seen him, and then again retreated into the shadow. In a moment the old servant was at his side.

THE WHITE MICE

"Is she here?" demanded Roddy.

Appreciating that in the world there could be only one "she," the little man nodded violently.

"Tell her," whispered Roddy, "I have seen her father, that he knows what we are trying to do. I must talk with the *señorita* at once. Ask her if she will come to the steps leading from the gardens to the wharf at any hour this evening. From my own house I can row there without being seen."

Again Pedro nodded happily.

"I will ask the *señorita* to be there at nine o'clock," he answered, "or, I will come myself."

The alternative did not strongly appeal to Roddy, but the mere fact that Inez was now in the same city with him, that even at that moment she was not a hundred yards from him, was in itself a reward.

He continued on down the Alameda, his head in the air, his feet treading on springs.

"Three hours!" his mind protested. "How can I wait three hours?"

In some fashion the hours passed, and at nine, just as over all the city the bugles were recalling the soldiers to the barracks, Roddy was waiting on the narrow stretch of beach that ran between the harbor and the gardens of Miramar.

VI

AT the last moment Roddy had decided against taking the water route, and, leaving his rowboat at his own wharf, had, on foot, skirted the edge of the harbor. It was high tide, and the narrow strip of shore front on which he now stood, and which ran between the garden and the Rojas' private wharf, was only a few feet in width. Overhead the moon was shining brilliantly, but a procession of black clouds caused the stone steps and the tiny summer-house at the end of the wharf to appear and disappear like slides in a magic lantern.

In one of the moments of light the figures of a man and a woman loomed suddenly in the gateway of the garden. Pedro came anxiously forward, and Roddy leaped past him up the steps. He recognized Inez with difficulty. In the fashion of the peasant women she had drawn around her head and face a fringed, silk shawl, which left only her eyes visible, and which hung from her shoulders in lines that hid her figure. Roddy eagerly stretched out his hand, but the girl raised her own in warning and, motioning him to follow, passed quickly from the steps to the wharf. At its farther end was a shelter of thatched palm leaves. The sides were open, and half of the wharf was filled with moonlight, but over the other half the roof cast a black shadow, and into this Inez passed quickly. Roddy as quickly followed. His heart was leaping in a delightful tumult. His love of adventure, of the picturesque, was deeply gratified. As he saw it, the scene was set for romance; he was once more in the presence of the girl who, though he had but twice met her, and, in spite of the fact that she had promised herself to another man, attracted him more strongly than had any woman he had ever known. And the tiny wharf, the lapping of the waves against the stone sides, the moonlight, the purpose of their meeting, all seemed combined for sentiment, for a display of the more tender emotions.

But he was quickly disillusionized. The voice that issued from the shadows was brisk and incisive.

"You know," Inez began abruptly, in sharp disapprobation, "this won't do at all!"

Had she pushed him into the cold waters of the harbor and left him to the colder charity of the harbor sharks, Roddy could not have been more completely surprised. He stared at the cloaked figure blankly.

THE WHITE MICE

"I *beg* your pardon!" he stammered.

"You must not expect me to meet you like this," protested the girl; "it is impossible. You risk everything."

Bewildered by the nature and the unexpectedness of the attack, Roddy murmured incoherently:

"I'm *so* sorry," he stammered. "I thought you would wish to know."

"What else is there I could so much wish!" protested the girl with spirit. "But not in this way."

Roddy hung his head humbly.

"I see," he murmured. "I forgot etiquette. I should have considered you."

"I was not thinking of myself!" exclaimed the girl. "A week ago I *was* frightened. Tradition, training, was strong with me, and I *did* think too much of how my meeting you would appear to others. But now I see it as you see it. I'll risk their displeasure, gossip, scandal, all of that, if I can only help my father. But *this* will not help him. This will lead to discovery. You must not come near me, nor visit this house. My mother"— the girl hesitated—"it is hard to say," she went on quickly, "but my mother more than dislikes you—she regards you as our evil genius. She thinks you are doing all in your power to spoil the

THE WHITE MICE

plans of your own father and of Vega. She—we have all heard of your striking Vega in defense of Alvarez. Vega is the one man she thinks can save my father. She believes you are his enemy. Therefore, you are her enemy. And she has been told, also, of the words you used to my father when your friend was permitted to visit him." With an effort the girl tried to eliminate from her voice the note of obvious impatience. "Of course," she added quickly, "the story came to us distorted. I could not see your object, but I was sure you had a motive. I was sure it was well meant!"

"Well meant!" exclaimed Roddy, but interrupted himself quickly. "All right," he said, "go on."

The girl recognized the restraint in his tone. "You think I am unjust, ungrateful," she protested earnestly, "but, believe me, I am not. I want only to impress upon you to be careful and to show you where you stand."

"With whom?" asked Roddy.

"With my mother and Vega and with their party."

"I am more interested," said Roddy, "in knowing how I stand with you."

The girl answered quietly: "Oh, we are friends. And you know that I am deeply

THE WHITE MICE

grateful to you because *I* know what you are trying to do, the others do not."

"Suppose we tell them?" said Roddy.

The girl gave a quick exclamation of protest, and Roddy could hear rather than see her move from him. They were now quite alone. Lest any one coming from the house should discover Roddy, Pedro had been on guard at the gate. But he had seen, both above and below the wharf, mysterious, moonlit figures loitering at the edge of the water, and in order to investigate them he left his post. There was a moment of silence. On three sides the moonlight turned the tiny waves into thousands of silver mirrors, and from farther up the curving coast-line the fires in the wicker-work huts of the fishermen burned red. At their feet the water was thick with the phosphorescence, shining more brilliantly than the moonlight. And, as schools of minnows fled, darting and doubling on their course before some larger fish that leaped and splashed in pursuit, the black depths of the harbor were lit with vivid streaks, and the drops of water cast into the air flashed like sparks from an anvil.

A harbor shark, nosing up stealthily to the wharf, thought himself invisible, but the phosphorescence showed his great length and cruel head as clearly as though he wore a suit of flame.

THE WHITE MICE

"Suppose you tell them?" repeated Roddy. The girl spoke with evident reluctance.

"I cannot," she said, "and the reason why I cannot is quite foolish, absurd. But their minds are full of it. In some way Vega learned of our meeting. He believes it was by accident, but, nevertheless, he also believes—why I can't imagine—that you are interested in me."

As though fearful Roddy would speak, she continued quickly. She spoke in impersonal, matter-of-fact tones that suggested that in the subject at hand she herself was in no way involved.

"My mother was already prejudiced against you because she thought that, for the sake of adventure, you were risking the life of my father. And this last suggestion of Vega's has added to her prejudice."

As though waiting for Roddy to make some comment or ask some question, the girl hesitated.

"I see," said Roddy.

"No, I am afraid you cannot see," said Inez, "unless you know the facts. I am sorry to weary you with family secrets, but, if you know them, my mother's prejudice is more easy to understand. Colonel Vega wishes to marry me. My mother also desires it. That is why they are hostile to you."

THE WHITE MICE

The young girl gave an exclamation of impatience.

"It is ridiculous," she protested, "that such an absurd complication should be brought into a matter of life and death. But there it is. And for that reason it would be folly to tell them of your purpose. They would accept nothing from your hands. You must continue to work alone, and you must not come near me nor try to speak to me. If it is absolutely necessary to communicate with me, write what you have to tell me; or, better still, give a verbal message to Pedro." She made an abrupt movement. "I must go!" she exclaimed. "I told them I would walk in the garden, and they may follow."

At the thought she gave a little gasp of alarm.

"Surely it is not as serious as that?" Roddy objected.

"Quite," returned the girl. "To them, what I am doing now is unpardonable. But I was afraid to write you. A letter may sound so harsh, it can be so easily misread. I did not wish to offend you, so I risked seeing you this way—for the last time."

"For the last time," repeated Roddy.

Inez made a movement to go.

"Wait!" he commanded. "Do you come often to this place?"

"Yes," said the girl, and then, answering the possible thought back of the question, she added: "My mother and sister come here with me every evening—for the sake of the harbor breeze—at least we used to do so. Why?" she demanded.

In her voice was a note of warning.

"I was thinking," said Roddy, "I could row past here in my boat, far out, where no one could see me. But I could see you."

Inez gave a quick sigh of exasperation.

"You will *not* understand!" she exclaimed. "Why," she demanded, "after all I have told you, after my taking this risk to make it plain to you that you must *not* see me, do you still persist?"

"As you wish," answered Roddy quietly, but his tone showed that his purpose to see her was unchanged. Inez heard him laugh happily. He moved suddenly toward her. "Why do I persist?" he asked. His voice, sunken to a whisper, was eager, mocking. In it she discerned a new note. It vibrated with feeling. "Why do I persist?" he whispered. "Because you are the most wonderful person I have ever met. Because if I did not persist I'd despise myself. Since I last saw you I have thought of nothing but *you*, I have been miserable for the sight of you. You can forbid me seeing you, but you can't take away from me what you have given me—the things you never knew you gave me."

The girl interrupted him sharply.

"Mr. Forrester!" she cried.

Roddy went on, as though she had not spoken.

"I had to tell you," he exclaimed. "Until I told you I couldn't sleep. It has been in my head, in my heart, every moment since I saw you. You *had* to know. And this night!" he exclaimed. As though calling upon them to justify him he flung out his arms toward the magic moonlight, the flashing waves, the great fronds of the palms rising above the wall of the garden. "You have given me," he cried, "the most beautiful thing that has come into my life, and on a night like this I *had* to speak. I had to thank you. On such a night as this," Roddy cried breathlessly, "Jessica stole from Shylock's house to meet her lover. On such a night as this Leander swam the Hellespont. And on this night I had to tell you that to me you are the most wonderful and beautiful woman in the world."

How Inez Rojas, bewildered, indignant, silent only through astonishment, would have met this attack, Roddy never knew, for Pedro, leaping suddenly from the shore, gave her no time to answer. Trembling with excitement, the Venezuelan spoke rapidly.

"You must go!" he commanded. He seized Roddy by the arm and tried to drag him toward the garden. "The police! They surround the house."

With his free hand he pointed at two figures, each carrying a lantern, who approached rapidly along the shore from either direction.

"They are spying upon all who enter. If they find *you!*" In an agony of alarm the old man tossed up his hands.

Under his breath Roddy cursed himself impotently for a fool. He saw that again he would compromise the girl he had just told he held in high regard, that he would put in jeopardy the cause for which he had boasted to her he would give his life. Furious, and considering only in what way he could protect Inez, he stood for a moment at a loss. From either side the swinging lanterns drew nearer. In his rear his retreat was cut off by the harbor. Only the dark shadows of Miramar offered a refuge.

"Quick!" commanded Inez. "You must hide in the garden." Her voice was cold with displeasure. "When they have gone Pedro will tell you and you will leave. And," she added, "you will see that you do not return."

The words sobered Roddy. They left him

On such a night . . . Leander swam the Hellespont.

THE WHITE MICE

smarting, and they left him quite cool. After her speech he could not accept the hospitality of the garden. And his hiding there might even further compromise her. He saw only one way out; to rush the nearest policeman and in the uncertain light, hope, unrecognized, to escape. But even that chance left the police free to explain, in their own way, why the Señorita Rojas was in the company of a man who fled before them.

"Do you hear?" whispered Inez. "Hide yourself!"

With a cry of dismay Pedro forced Roddy into the shadow.

"It is too late!" he exclaimed.

Standing in the gateway of the garden, clearly illuminated by the moonlight, stood Señora Rojas, with her arm in that of Pino Vega.

In spite of himself, Roddy emitted an excited chuckle. In the presence of such odds his self-reproaches fell from him. He felt only a pleasing thrill of danger. This was no time for regrets or upbraidings. The situation demanded of him only quick action and that he should keep his head. As Roddy now saw it, he was again the base-runner, beset in front and rear. He missed only the shouts and cheers of thousands of partisans. The players of the other side were closing in and shortening the distance in which he could turn and run. They had him in a trap, and, in another instant, the ball would touch him. It was quite time, Roddy decided, to "slide!" Still hidden by the shadow of the thatched roof, he dropped at the feet of Inez, and, before she could understand his purpose, had turned quickly on his face and lowered himself into the harbor. There was a faint splash and a shower of phosphorescence. Roddy's fingers still clung to the edge of the wharf, and Inez, sinking to her knees, brought her face close to his.

"Come back!" she commanded. "Come back! You will drown!" She gave a sudden gasp of horror. "The sharks!" she whispered. "You could not live a moment." With both hands she dragged at his sleeve.

Roddy cast a quick glance at the moon. A friendly cloud was hastening to his aid. He saw that if, for a moment longer, he could remain concealed, he would under cover of the brief eclipse, be able to swim to safety. He drew free of Inez, and, treading water, fearful even to breathe, watched the lanterns of the police halt at the wharf.

The voice of Señora Rojas rose in anxious inquiry.

"Is that you, Inez?" she called.

There was no reply. Concerned as to what

THE WHITE MICE

struggle of conscience might not be going on in the mind of the girl, Roddy threw his arm across the edge of the wharf and drew his shoulders clear of the water. In the shadow Inez was still kneeling, her face was still close to his.

"Answer her!" commanded Roddy. "I'm all right." He laughed softly, mockingly. He raised his head nearer. "'On such a night,'" he whispered, "'Leander swam the Hellespont.' Why? Because he loved her!"

With an exclamation, partly of exasperation, partly of relief at finding the man did not consider himself in danger, Inez rose to her feet and stepped into the moonlight.

"Yes, I am here," she called. "I am with Pedro."

At the same moment the black cloud swept across the moon, and, with the stealth and silence of a water rat, Roddy slipped from the wharf and struck out toward the open harbor.

At the gate the two policemen raised their lanterns and swung them in the face of Señora Rojas.

Vega turned upon them fiercely.

"What are you doing here?" he demanded. "Do you wish to know who I am? Well, I am Colonel Vega. Report that to your chief. Go!"

THE WHITE MICE

With a gesture he waved the men to one side, and, saluting sulkily, they moved away.

When they had gone Señora Rojas sighed with relief, but the hand that rested upon the arm of Vega trembled.

"My dear lady!" he protested. "When I am here no harm can come."

Vega hoped that Inez had heard him. He trusted, also, that she had observed the manner in which he had addressed the police, and how, awed by his authority, they had slunk away. But Inez had not observed him.

With her hands pressed against her breast, her eyes filled with fear, she was watching in fascinated horror a thin ripple of phosphorescence that moved leisurely and steadily out to sea.

. . . .

In the *patio* of Roddy's house Peter was reclining in a steamer-chair. At his elbow was a long drink, and between his fingers a long cigar. Opposite him, in another chair, was stretched young Vicenti. At midnight, on his way home from visiting a patient, the doctor, seeing a light in the court-yard of Roddy's house, had clamored for admittance. To Peter the visit was most ill-timed. Roddy had now been absent for four hours, and the imagina-

THE WHITE MICE

tion of his friend was greatly disturbed. He knew for what purpose Roddy had set forth, and he pictured him pierced with a bullet as he climbed the garden wall, or a prisoner behind the bars of the *cartel*. He was in no mood to entertain visitors, but the servants were in bed, and when Vicenti knocked, Peter himself had opened the door. On any other night the doctor would have been most welcome. He was an observing young man, and his residence in the States enabled him to take the point of view of Peter and Roddy, and his comments upon their country and his own were amusing. For his attack upon General Rojas he had been greatly offended with Roddy, but the American had written him an apology, and by this late and informal visit Vicenti intended to show that they were again friends.

But, for Peter, it was a severe test of self-control. Each moment his fears for Roddy's safety increased, and of his uneasiness, in the presence of the visitor, he dared give no sign. It was with a feeling of genuine delight that he heard from the garden a mysterious whistle.

"Who's there?" he challenged.

"Is anybody with you?" The voice was strangely feeble, but it was the voice of Roddy.

"Our friend Vicenti," Peter cried, warningly.

At the same moment, Roddy, clad simply in his stockings, and dripping with water, stood swaying in the doorway.

"For Heaven's sake!" protested Peter.

Roddy grinned foolishly, and unclasping his hands from the sides of the door, made an unsteady start toward the table on which stood the bottles and glasses.

"I want a drink," he murmured.

"You want quinine!" cried Vicenti indignantly. "How dared you go swimming at night! It was madness! If the fever——"

He flew into the hall where he had left his medicine-case, and Peter ran for a bath-robe. As they returned with them there was a crash of broken glass, and when they reached the *patio* they found Roddy stretched at length upon the stones.

At the same moment a little, old man sprang from the garden and knelt beside him. It was Pedro.

"He is dead!" he cried, "he is dead!"

His grief was so real that neither Peter nor Vicenti could suppose he was other than a friend, and without concerning himself as to how he had been so suddenly precipitated into the scene, Vicenti, as he poured brandy between Roddy's teeth, commanded Pedro to rub and beat his body. Coughing and choking, Roddy

THE WHITE MICE

signalized his return to consciousness by kicking the little man in the stomach.

"Ah, he lives!" cried Pedro. He again dropped upon his knees and, crossing himself, prayed his thanks.

Roddy fell into the bath-robe and into the steamer-chair. Sighing luxuriously, he closed his eyes.

"Such a fool, to faint," he murmured. "So ashamed. Made a bet—with harbor sharks. Bet them, could not get me. I win." He opened his eyes and stared dully at Pedro. "Hello!" he said, "there's good old Pedro. What you doing here, Pedro?"

The old man, now recovered from his fear on Roddy's account, was in fresh alarm as to his own, and, glancing at Vicenti, made a movement to escape into the garden.

Roddy waved Vicenti and Peter into the hall.

"Go away," he commanded. "He wants to talk to me."

"But I must not leave you," protested the doctor. "Now I am here as your physician, not as your guest."

"A moment," begged Roddy, "a moment." His eyes closed and his head fell back. Pedro bent over him.

"She sent me," he whispered eagerly. "She could not sleep. She must know to-night if

THE WHITE MICE

you live. I hid myself in your garden, and I wait and I wait. But you do not come, and I despair. And then," cried the old man joyfully, "the miracle! Now my mistress can sleep in peace."

Roddy lay so still that had it not been for his sharp breathing Pedro would have thought he had again fainted. With a sudden, sharp cry Roddy opened his eyes. His clinched fists beat feebly on the arms of the chair.

"It's a lie!" he shouted fiercely, "it's a lie!" His eyes were wide and staring. Vicenti, returning hastily, looked into them and, with an exclamation, drew back.

"The fever!" he said.

Roddy was shouting wildly.

"It's a lie!" he cried. "She did *not* send you. She does not care whether I drown or live. She loves Pino Vega. She will marry——"

Peter, with his arm around Roddy's neck, choked him, and held his hand over his mouth.

"Be still," he entreated, "for God's sake, be still!" He looked fearfully at Vicenti, but the young doctor, though his eyes were wide with astonishment, made an impatient gesture.

"Help me get him to bed," Vicenti commanded briskly. "Take his other arm."

With the strength the fever lent him, Roddy hurled the two men from him.

THE WHITE MICE

"She and Vega—they stood on the wharf," he shouted, "you understand? They laughed at me. And then the sharks smelt me out and followed; and I couldn't hide because the harbor was on fire. I struck at them and screamed, but I couldn't shake them off; they dived and turned; they crept up on me stealthily, in great circles. They were waiting for me to drown. Whichever way I swam I saw them, under me, on every side! They lit the water with great streaks of flame. And she and Vega pointed me out and laughed."

"Stop him!" shrieked Peter. "You *must not* listen! Give him morphine! Dope him! Stop him!"

Roddy wrenched his wrists free and ran to Pedro, clutching him by the shoulders.

"But *we'll* save him!" he cried. "*We'll* set him free! Because he is an old man. Because he is a great man. Because he is her father. We'll make him President!" His voice soared exultantly. "To hell with Vega!" he shouted. "To hell with Alvarez!" He flung up his arms into the air. "Viva Rojas!" he cried.

Peter turned on Vicenti and shook his fist savagely in his face.

"What you've heard," he threatened, "you've heard under the seal of your profession."

But the eyes that looked into his were as

THE WHITE MICE

wild as those of the man driven with fever. The face of the Venezuelan was jubilant, exalted, like that of a worshipping fanatic.

"The truth!" he whispered breathlessly, "the truth!"

"The boy is raving mad," protested Peter. "He doesn't mean it. You have heard nothing!"

From the servants' quarters there came the sound of hurrying footsteps.

In alarm, Vicenti glanced in that direction, and then came close to Peter, seizing him by the arm.

"If he's mad," he whispered fiercely, "then *I* am mad, and I know ten thousand more as mad as he."

When the sun rose dripping out of the harbor, Vicenti and Peter walked into the garden.

"I can leave him now," said the doctor. He looked at Peter's white face and the black rings around his eyes, and laughed. "When he wakes," he said, "he will be in much better health than you or I."

"He certainly gave us a jolly night," sighed Peter, "and I shall never thank you enough for staying by me and Pedro. When a man I've roomed with for two years can't make up his mind whether I am I or a shark, it gets on my nerves."

THE WHITE MICE

A few hours later, in another garden half a mile distant, Pedro was telling his young mistress of the night just past. The tears stood in his eyes and his hands trembled in eloquent pantomime.

"He is so like my young master, your brother," he pleaded, "so brave, so strong, so young, and, like him, loves so deeply."

"I am very grateful," said the girl gently. "For my father and for me he risked his life. I am grateful to him—and to God, who spared him."

Pedro lowered his eyes as he repeated: "And he loves so deeply."

The girl regarded him steadily.

"What is it you wish to say?" she demanded.

"All through the night I sat beside him," answered the old man eagerly, "and in his fever he spoke only one name."

The girl turned from him and for a moment stood looking out into the harbor.

"Then the others heard?" she said.

Pedro, with a deprecatory gesture, bowed. With sudden vehemence, with a gesture of relief, the girl flung out her arms.

"I'm glad," she cried. "I am *tired* of secrets, tired of deceit. I am glad they know. It makes me proud! It makes me happy!"

During the long night, while Roddy had

tossed and muttered, Vicenti talked to Peter frankly and freely. He held back nothing. His appointment as prison doctor he had received from Alvarez, but it was impossible for any one to be long in close contact with General Rojas and not learn to admire and love him. And for the past year Vicenti had done all in his power to keep life in the older man and to work for his release. But General Rojas, embittered by past experience, did not confide in him, did not trust him. In spite of this, the doctor had continued working in his interests. He assured Peter that the adherents of Rojas were many, that they were well organized, that they waited only for the proper moment to revolt against Alvarez, release Rojas, and place him in power. On their programme Vega had no place. They suspected his loyalty to his former patron and chief, they feared his ambition; and they believed, were he to succeed in making himself President, he would be the servant of Forrester, and of the other foreigners who desired concessions, rather than of the people of Venezuela. The amnesty, Vicenti believed, had been declared only that Alvarez might entice Vega to Venezuela, where, when he wished, he could lay his hands on him. When he had obtained evidence that Vega was plotting against him he would submit this

THE WHITE MICE

evidence to the people and throw Vega into prison.

"Vega knows his danger," added Vicenti, "and, knowing it, he must mean to strike soon—to-day—to-morrow. We of the Rojas faction are as ignorant of his plans as we hope he is of ours. But in every camp there are traitors. No one can tell at what hour all our secrets may not be made known. Of only one thing you can be certain: matters cannot continue as they are. Within a week you will see this country torn by civil war, or those who oppose Alvarez, either of our party or of Vega's, will be in prison."

When Roddy, rested and refreshed and with normal pulse and mind, came to luncheon, Peter confided to him all that Vicenti had told him.

"If all that is going to happen," was Roddy's comment, "the sooner we get Rojas free the better. We will begin work on the tunnel to-night."

The attacking party consisted of McKildrick, Roddy, and Peter. When the day's task on the light-house was finished and the other workmen had returned to the city, these three men remained behind and, placing crowbars, picks, and sticks of dynamite in Roddy's launch, proceeded to a little inlet a half-mile below El

Morro. By seven o'clock they had made their way through the laurel to the fortress, and while Roddy and Peter acted as lookouts McKildrick attacked the entrance to the tunnel. He did not, as he had boasted, open it in an hour, but by ten o'clock the iron bars that held the slabs together had been cut and the cement loosened. Fearful of the consequences if they returned to the city at too late an hour, the tools and dynamite were hidden, rubbish and vines were so scattered as to conceal the evidence of their work, and the launch landed the conspirators at Roddy's wharf.

"We shall say," explained Roddy, "that we have been out spearing eels, and I suggest that we now go to the *Dos Hermanos* and say it."

They found the café, as usual, crowded. Men of all political opinions, officers of the army and the custom-house, from the tiny warship in the harbor, Vegaistas, and those who secretly were adherents of Rojas, were all gathered amicably together. The Americans, saluting impartially their acquaintances, made their way to a table that remained empty in the middle of the room. They had hardly seated themselves when from a distant corner an alert young man, waving his hand in greeting, pushed his way toward them. They recog-

THE WHITE MICE

nized the third vice-president of the Forrester Construction Company, Mr. Sam Caldwell.

Mr. Caldwell had arrived that afternoon. He was delighted at being free of the ship. At the house of Colonel Vega he had dined well, and at sight of familiar faces he was inclined to unbend. He approached the employees of the company as one conferring a favor and assured of a welcome. He appreciated that since his arrival he was the man of the moment. In the crowded restaurant every one knew him as the representative of that great corporation that had dared to lock horns with the government. As he passed the tables the officers of that government followed him with a scowl or a sneer; those of the Vegaistas, who looked upon him as the man who dealt out money, ammunition and offices, with awe. How the secret supporters of Rojas considered him was soon to appear.

"This," Roddy whispered in a quick aside, "is where I renounce the F. C. C. and all its works."

"Don't be an ass!" entreated Peter.

Roddy rose and, with his hands sunk in his pockets, awaited the approach of the third vice-president.

"Well, boys, here I am!" called that young man heartily. He seemed to feel that his own surprise at finding himself outside the limits of Greater New York must be shared by all. But, as though to see to whom this greeting was extended, Roddy turned and glanced at his companions.

McKildrick rose and stood uncomfortably.

"Well, Roddy," exclaimed Sam Caldwell genially, "how's business?"

Roddy's eyebrows rose.

"'Roddy?'" he repeated, as though he had not heard aright. "Are you speaking to me?"

Sam Caldwell was conscious that over all the room there had come a sudden hush. A waiter, hurrying with a tray of jingling glasses, by some unseen hand was jerked by the apron and brought to abrupt silence. In the sudden quiet Roddy's voice seemed to Caldwell to have come through a megaphone. The pink, smooth-shaven cheeks of the newcomer, that were in such contrast to the dark and sun-tanned faces around him, turned slowly red.

"What's the idea?" he asked.

"You sent me a cable to Curaçao," Roddy replied, "telling me to mind my own business."

It had never been said of Sam Caldwell that he was an unwilling or unworthy antagonist. He accepted Roddy's challenge promptly. His little, piglike eyes regarded Roddy contemptuously.

THE WHITE MICE

"I did," he retaliated, "at your father's dictation."

"Well, my business hours," continued Roddy undisturbed, "are between eight and five. If you come out to the light-house to-morrow you will see me minding my own business and bossing a gang of niggers, at twenty dollars a week. Outside of business hours I choose my own company."

Caldwell came closer to him and dropped his voice.

"Are you sober?" he demanded.

"Perfectly," said Roddy.

Caldwell surveyed him grimly.

"You are more out of hand than we thought," he commented. "I have heard some pretty strange tales about you this afternoon. Are they true?"

"You have your own methods of finding out," returned Roddy. He waved his hand toward the table. "If you wish to join these gentlemen I am delighted to withdraw."

Caldwell retreated a few steps and then turned back angrily.

"I'll have a talk with you to-morrow," he said, "and to-night I'll cable your father what you are doing here."

Roddy bowed and slightly raised his voice, so that it reached to every part of the room.

"If you can interest my father," he said, "in anything that concerns his son I shall be grateful."

As Caldwell made his way to the door, and Roddy, frowning gravely, sank back into his chair, the long silence was broken by a babble of whispered questions and rapid answers. Even to those who understood no English the pantomime had been sufficiently enlightening. Unobtrusively the secret agents of Alvarez rose from the tables and stole into the night. A half-hour later it was known in Caracas that the son of Mr. Forrester had publicly insulted the representative of his father, the arch-enemy of the government, and had apparently ranged himself on the side of Alvarez. Hitherto the *Dos Hermanos* had been free from politics, but as Roddy made his exit from the café, the officers of the army chose the moment for a demonstration. Revolution was in the air, and they desired to declare their loyalty. Rising to their feet and raising their glasses to Roddy they cried, "Bravo, bravo! Viva Alvarez!"

Bowing and nodding to them and wishing them good-night, Roddy hurried to the street.

Under the lamps of the Alameda McKildrick regarded him quizzically.

"And what do you gain by that?" he asked.

"Well, I force Sam into the open," declared

THE WHITE MICE

Roddy, "and I'm no longer on the suspect list. Look at my record! I've insulted everybody. I have insulted Rojas, insulted Vega, insulted Caldwell, all enemies of Alvarez. So now the Alvarez crowd will love me. Now they trust me! If they caught me digging the tunnel and I told them I was building a lighthouse, they'd believe me. If I insult a few more people they'll give me the Order of Bolivar."

The next morning Roddy attended Mass. But he was not entirely engrossed in his devotions. Starting from the front entrance of the church he moved slowly nearer and nearer to the altar, and, slipping from the shelter of one pillar to another, anxiously scanned the rows of kneeling women. He found the mantilla a baffling disguise, and as each woman present in the church wore one, and as the hair of each was black, and as the back of the head of one woman is very much like that of another, it was not until the worshippers had turned to leave that he discovered the Señorita Inez Rojas. In her black satin dress, with her face wreathed by the black lace mantilla, Roddy thought he had never seen her look more beautiful.

After her explicit commands that he should not attempt to see her again he was most anxious she should not learn how soon he had

THE WHITE MICE

disobeyed her; and that she was walking with her sister and mother made it still more necessary that he should remain unnoticed.

But in his eagerness and delight in the sight of her he leaned far forward. Inez, at that instant raising her eyes, saw him. Of the two Roddy was the more concerned. The girl made no sign of recognition, but the next moment, with an exclamation, she suddenly unclasped her hands, and, as though to show they were empty, held them toward her mother and sister. Leaving them, she returned hurriedly toward the altar. Señora Rojas and the sister continued on their way toward the door, exchanging greetings with the women of their acquaintance, whom, after an absence of two years, they now met for the first time. Seeing them thus engaged Inez paused and, turning, looked directly at Roddy. Her glance was not forbidding, and Roddy, who needed but little encouragement, hastened to follow. The church was very dark. The sunlight came only through the lifted curtains at the farthest entrance, and the acolytes were already extinguishing the candles that had illuminated the altar. As Inez, in the centre of the church, picked her way among the scattered praying-chairs, Roddy, in the side aisle and hidden by the pillars, kept pace with her.

THE WHITE MICE

Directly in front of the altar Inez stooped, and, after picking up a fan and a prayer-book, stood irresolutely looking about her. Roddy cautiously emerged from the side aisle and from behind the last of the long row of pillars. Inez came quickly toward him. The last of the acolytes to leave the altar, in their haste to depart, stumbled and tripped past them, leaving them quite alone. Concealed by the great pillar from all of those in the far front of the church, Inez gave Roddy her hand. The eyes that looked into his were serious, penitent.

"I am so sorry," she begged; "can you forgive me?"

"Forgive you!" whispered Roddy. His voice was filled with such delight that it was apparently a sufficient answer. Inez, smiling slightly, withdrew her hand, and taking from inside her glove a folded piece of paper, thrust it toward him.

"I brought this for you," she said.

Roddy seized it greedily.

"For me!" he exclaimed in surprise. As though in apology for the question he raised his eyes appealingly. "How did you know," he begged, "that I would be here?"

For an instant, with a frown, the girl regarded him steadily. Then her cheeks flushed slightly and her eyes grew radiant. She flashed upon him the same mocking, dazzling smile that twice before had left him in complete subjection.

"How did you know," she returned, "*I* would be here?"

She moved instantly from him, but Roddy started recklessly in pursuit.

"Wait!" he demanded. "Just what does that mean?"

With an imperative gesture the girl motioned him back, and then, as though to soften the harshness of the gesture, reassured him in a voice full of consideration.

"The note will tell you," she whispered, and, turning her back on him, hurried to the door.

Roddy allowed her sufficient time in which to leave the neighborhood of the church, and while he waited, as the most obvious method of expressing his feelings, stuffed all the coins in his pockets into the poor-box. From the church he hastened to an empty bench in the Alameda, and opened the note. He was surprised to find that it came from Mrs. Broughton, the wife of the English Consul at Porto Cabello. She was an American girl who, against the advice of her family, had married an Englishman, and one much older than herself. Since their marriage he had indulged and

THE WHITE MICE

spoiled her as recklessly as any American might have done, and at the same time, in his choice of a wife, had continued to consider himself a most fortunate individual. Since his arrival at Porto Cabello Roddy had been a friend of each. For hours he would play in the garden with their children, without considering it necessary to inform either the father or mother that he was on the premises; and on many evenings the Broughtons and himself sat in his *patio* reading the American periodicals, without a word being spoken by any one of them until they said good-night. But since his return from Curaçao, Roddy had been too occupied with coming events to remember old friends.

The note read:

DEAR MR. FORRESTER: My husband and I have not seen you for ages, and the children cry for "Uncle Roddy." Will you and Mr. De Peyster take tea with us day after to-morrow? The only other friend who is coming *will give you this note.*

The Broughtons had been stationed at Porto Cabello for five years, and, as Roddy now saw, it was most natural that in the limited social life of Porto Cabello the two American girls should be friends. That he had not already thought of the possibility of this filled him with rage, and, at the same time, the promise held forth by the note thrilled him with pleasure. He leaped to his feet and danced jubilantly upon the gravel walk. Tearing the note into scraps he hurled them into the air.

"Mary Broughton!" he exclaimed ecstatically, "you're a brick!"

Such was his feeling of gratitude to the lady, that he at once sought out a confectioner's and sent her many pounds of the candied fruits that have made Venezuela famous, and that, on this occasion, for several days made the Broughton children extremely ill.

That night the attack on the barricade to the tunnel was made with a vigor no cement nor rusty iron could resist. Inspired by the thought that on the morrow he would see Inez, and that she herself wished to see him, and anxious to give her a good report of the work of rescue, Roddy toiled like a coal-passer. His energy moved McKildrick and Peter to endeavors equally strenuous, and by nine o'clock the great stone slabs were wedged apart, and on the warm-scented night air and upon the sweating bodies of the men there struck a cold, foul breath that told them one end of the tunnel lay open.

VII

Roddy was for at once dashing down the stone steps and exploring the tunnel, but McKildrick held him back.

"You couldn't live for a moment," he protested, "and it may be days before we can enter." In proof of what he said, he lit one wax match after another, and as he passed each over the mouth of the tunnel Roddy saw the flame sicken and die.

"That has been a tomb for half a century," McKildrick reminded him. "Even if a strong, young idiot like you could breathe that air, Rojas couldn't."

"All the same, I am going down," said Roddy.

"And I tell you, you are not!" returned McKildrick.

Roddy, jubilant and grandly excited, laughed mockingly.

"'Am *I* the Governor of these Isles, or is it an Emilio Aguinaldo?'" he demanded. "This is *my* expedition, and I speak to lead the forlorn hope."

THE WHITE MICE

Exclaiming with impatience, McKildrick brought a rope and, making a noose, slipped it under Roddy's arms.

"All we ask," he said grimly, "is that when you faint you'll fall with your head toward us. Otherwise we will bump it into a jelly."

Roddy switched on the light in his electric torch and, like a diver descending a sea-ladder, moved cautiously down the stone steps. Holding the rope taut, Peter leaned over the opening.

"When the snakes and bats and vampires get you," he warned, "you'll wish you were back among the sharks!"

But Roddy did not hear him. As though warding off a blow he threw his hands across his face and dropped heavily.

"Heave!" cried Peter.

The two men sank their heels in the broken rubbish and dragged on the rope until they could lay violent hands on Roddy's shoulders. With unnecessary roughness they pulled him out of the opening and let him fall.

When Roddy came to he rose sheepishly.

"We'll have to postpone that expedition," he said, "until we can count on better ventilation. Meanwhile, if any gentleman wants to say, 'I told you so,' I'll listen to him."

They replaced the slabs over the mouth of

the tunnel, but left wide openings through which the air and sunlight could circulate, and, after concealing these openings with vines, returned to Roddy's house. There they found Vicenti awaiting them. He was the bearer of important news. The adherents of Colonel Vega, he told them, were assembling in force near Porto Cabello, and it was well understood by the government that at any moment Vega might join them and proclaim his revolution. That he was not already under arrest was due to the fact that the government wished to seize not only the leader, but all of those who were planning to leave the city with him. The home of Vega was surrounded, and he himself, in his walks abroad, closely guarded. That he would be able to escape seemed all but impossible.

"At the same time," continued Vicenti, "our own party is in readiness. If Vega reaches his followers and starts on his march to the capital we will start an uprising here in favor of Rojas. If we could free Rojas and show him to the people, nothing could save Alvarez. Alvarez knows that as well as ourselves. But without artillery it is impossible to subdue the fortress of San Carlos. We can take this city; we can seize the barracks, the custom-house, but not San Carlos. There also is this danger: that

Alvarez, knowing without Rojas our party would fall to pieces, may at the first outbreak order him to be shot."

Roddy asked Vicenti, as the physician of Rojas, if he thought Rojas were strong enough to lead a campaign.

"He is not," declared Vicenti, "but we would not ask it of him. Let him only show himself and there will be no campaign. Even the government troops would desert to him. But," he added with a sigh, "why talk of the impossible! The troops that hold San Carlos are bound to Alvarez. He has placed there only those from his own plantation; he has paid them royally. And they have other reasons for fighting to the death. Since they have been stationed at Porto Cabello their conduct has been unspeakable. And the men of this town hate them as much as the women fear them. Their cruelty to the political prisoners is well known, and they understand that if an uprising started here where Rojas has lived, where he is dearly loved, they need expect no mercy. They will fight, not to protect San Carlos, but for their lives."

Vicenti spoke with such genuine feeling that had Roddy felt free to do so he would have told him of the plan to rescue Rojas. But both Peter and McKildrick had warned him

THE WHITE MICE

that until the last moment no one, save themselves, must learn the secret of the tunnel.

So, while they thanked Vicenti for his confidences, they separated for the night without having made him any return in kind.

The next morning, Sam Caldwell, under the guidance of McKildrick, paid an official visit to the light-house on which the men of the F. C. C. were then at work. When his tour of inspection was finished he returned to the wheel-house of the tug that had brought him across the harbor, and sent for Roddy. Roddy appeared before him in his working-clothes. They consisted of very few garments, and those were entirely concealed by the harbor mud. Caldwell, in cool, clean duck and a flamboyant Panama hat, signified with a grin that he enjoyed the contrast. He did not like Roddy, and Roddy treated him with open insolence. They were nearly of the same age and for years had known each other, but they had always been at war. As son of the president of the company, every chance had been given Roddy to advance his own interests. And it was not so much that he had failed to be of service to the company, as that he had failed to push himself forward, that caused Caldwell to regard him with easy contempt.

On his side, Roddy considered Caldwell the

bribe-giver and keeper of the corruption fund for the company, and, as such, beneath his royal notice. It therefore followed that in his present position of brief authority over Roddy, Caldwell found a certain enjoyment. This he concealed beneath the busy air of a man of affairs.

"I have a cable here from your father, Roddy," he began briskly. "Translated, the part that refers to you reads, 'Tell Forrester take orders from you or leave service company. If refuses, furnish return passage, month's wages.'"

After a pause, Roddy said: "I take it that is in answer to a cable from you."

"Exactly," assented Caldwell. "I informed your father you were insubordinate to my authority, and that I had been reliably informed you were hostile to our interests. What you do as an individual doesn't count for much, but as the son of your father, apparently down here at least, it does. Why you made that play at me last night I don't know, and I haven't time to find out. I am not here to teach you manners. But when you butt in and interfere with the business of the company I must take notice. You've either got to stop working against us, or go home. Which do you want to do? And before you answer," Caldwell added, "you ought to know that, as it is, you don't stand very high at headquarters. When your father got word you'd been fighting Vega, our friend, in defense of Alvarez, the man that's robbing us, that's giving us all this trouble, he was naturally pretty hot. He said to me: 'Roddy isn't down there to mix up in politics, but if he does, he must mix up on our side. I can't take money from the company to support my son, or any one else, who is against it.' That's what your father said to me. Now, as I understand it, although it is none of my business, you are dependent on him, and I advise——"

"As you say," interrupted Roddy, "it's none of your business. The other proposition," he went on, "that I can't take money from the company and work against it, is fair enough. What you call my work *against* it was begun before I knew it was in any way opposed to the company's interests. Now that I do know, I quite agree that either I must give up my outside job or quit working for you." Roddy reached to the shoulder of his flannel shirt, and meditatively began to unroll his damp and mud-soaked sleeve. "I guess I'll quit now!" he said.

The answer was not the one Caldwell expected or desired. As an employee of the company Roddy was not important, but what he was doing as an individual, which had so greatly excited Vega, was apparently of much importance. And what it might be Sam Caldwell was anxious to discover. He had enjoyed his moment of triumph and now adopted a tone more conciliatory.

"There's no use getting hot about it," he urged. "Better think it over."

Roddy nodded, and started to leave the wheel-house.

"Have thought it over," he said.

As Caldwell saw it, Roddy was acting from pique and in the belief that his father would continue to supply him with funds. This Caldwell knew was not the intention of Mr. Forrester. He had directed Caldwell to inform Roddy that if he deliberately opposed him he must not only seek work elsewhere, but that he did not think he should continue to ask his father for support. Caldwell proceeded to make this quite plain to Roddy, but, except that the color in his face deepened and that his jaw set more firmly, Roddy made no sign.

"Very well, then," concluded Caldwell, "you leave me no other course than to carry out your father's direction. I'll give you a month's wages and pay your passage-money home."

"I'm not going home," returned Roddy, "and I don't want any money I haven't worked for. The company isn't discharging me," he added with a grin, "as it would a cook. I am discharging the company."

"I warn you your father won't stand for it," protested Caldwell.

Roddy turned back, and in a serious tone, and emphasizing his words with a pointed forefinger, spoke earnestly.

"Sam," he said, "I give you my word, father is in wrong. *You* are in wrong. You're both backing the wrong stable. When this row starts your man Vega won't run one, two, three."

"You mean Rojas?" said Caldwell.

"I mean Rojas," replied Roddy. "And if you and father had trusted me I could have told you so three months ago. It would have saved you a lot of money. It isn't too late even now. You'd better listen to me."

Caldwell laughed comfortably.

"Rojas is a back number," he said. "He's an old man, and a dead one. And besides—" He hesitated and glanced away.

"Well?" demanded Roddy.

"And, besides," continued Caldwell slowly, picking his words, "Vega is going to marry his daughter, and so we win both ways. And Vega is amenable to reason. *He* will help us." As though in a sudden burst of confidence he added ingratiatingly, "And you could help your father, too, if you liked. If you'll tell me what the Rojas party mean to do I'll set you right with your father. What do you say?"

"What do I say, you poor, little—thing!" Roddy roared. Then he laughed shortly and shrugged his shoulders. "I'll say this much," he added. "If I were sure you couldn't swim I'd throw you into the harbor."

"So you could pull me out," laughed Caldwell. "Why don't you? You know you were always a grand-stand actor, Roddy. Think how heroic it would be," he taunted, "to rescue the hated enemy, to save my life!"

Roddy, unmoved, regarded him thoughtfully.

"It would be an awful thing to have on one's conscience," he said, and left the wheel-house.

When, at five o'clock that same afternoon, Roddy found himself sitting opposite Inez Rojas in a properly appointed drawing-room, guarded by a properly appointed chaperon and with a cup of tea on his knee, the situation struck him not only as delightful, but comic. With inward amusement he thought of their other meetings: those before sunrise, and the one by moonlight when Inez had told him he was seeing her for the last time, and when policemen threatened his advance and sharks cut off his retreat. From a smile in the eyes of

THE WHITE MICE

the girl herself Roddy guessed that she also found the meeting not without its humorous side. Roddy soon discovered he could not adjust his feelings to the exigencies of an afternoon call. After doing his duty as an adopted uncle to the Broughton children and to his hostess and her tea and to Peter, in permitting him ten minutes' talk with Inez, he brought that interview to an abrupt end.

"Miss Rojas," he exclaimed, "you haven't seen Mrs. Broughton's garden in two years, have you? Such a lot of things grow up in two years. Let me introduce them to you."

Giving her no chance to demur, Roddy strode out of the French windows into the garden, and, as Inez with an apologetic bow to the others followed, Peter moved to a chair beside Mrs. Broughton and held out his empty cup.

"There's a certain subtlety about Roddy's methods," he remarked, "that would easily deceive the deaf, dumb and blind."

The garden was full of rare trees, plants and flowers brought from every island of the Caribbean Sea, but Roddy did not pause to observe them. He led the way to a bench under a cluster of young bamboo trees and motioned to the girl to sit down. When she had done so he seated himself sideways on the bench and gazed at her. His eyes were filled with happiness.

"It's quite too wonderful to be true," he said contentedly.

Inez Rojas turned to the tropical splendor of the garden.

"Yes," she answered. "Everything grows so fast here. The change is quite wonderful."

Roddy shook his head at her disappointedly.

"You mustn't do that," he reproved her gravely; "when you know what I mean you mustn't pretend to think I mean something else. It's not honest. And time is too short. To me—these moments are too tremendously valuable. Every other time I have seen you I've had to keep looking over my shoulder for spies. Even now," he exclaimed in alarm, "those infernal Broughton children may find me and want to play ride-a-cock-horse! So you see," he went on eagerly, "you must not waste time misunderstanding me."

"Will you tell me about the tunnel?" asked the girl.

"The tunnel!" repeated Roddy blankly.

But he saw that her mind was occupied only with thoughts of her father, and at once, briskly and clearly, he explained to her all that had been accomplished, and all the plots and counterplots that were in the air.

"And how soon," asked the girl, "do you think it will be safe to enter the tunnel?"

THE WHITE MICE

Roddy answered that McKildrick thought in two or three days it would be clean of poisonous gases, but that that night they would again attempt to explore it.

"If I could only help!" exclaimed Inez. "It is not fair that strangers to my father should be taking a risk that should fall to one of his children. It would mean so much, it would make me so happy, if I could feel I had done any little thing for him. You cannot know how grateful I am to you all, to your friends, and to you!" Her eyes opened wide in sympathy. "And you were so ill," she exclaimed, "and the fever is so likely to return. I do not see how it is possible for you to work at night at El Morro and by day on the lighthouse and not break down. We have no right to permit it."

"My health," explained Roddy dryly, "is in no danger from overwork. I am not employed by the company any longer. If I like I can sleep all day. I've discharged myself. I've lost my job."

"You have quarrelled with your father," said the girl quickly, "on account of my father? You must not!" she exclaimed. "Indeed, we cannot accept such a sacrifice."

"The misunderstanding with my father," Roddy assured her, "is one of long standing.

I've never made a success of what he's given me to do, and this is only the last of a series of failures. You mustn't try to make me out an unselfish person. I am sacrificing nothing. Rather, in a way, I have gained my independence. At least, if I get a position now, people can't say I obtained it through my father's influence. Of course, it's awkward to be poor," added Roddy dispassionately, "because I had meant to ask you to marry me."

With an exclamation the girl partly rose and then sank back, retreating to the farthest limit of the bench.

"Mr. Forrester!" she began with spirit.

"I know what you're going to say," interrupted Roddy confidently. "But I ought to tell you that that doesn't weigh with me at all. I never could see," he exclaimed impatiently, 'why, if you love a girl, the fact that she is engaged should make any difference—do *you*? It is, of course, an obstacle, but if you are the right man, and the other man is not, it certainly is best for everybody that you should make that plain to her before she marries the wrong man. In your case it certainly has made no difference to me, and I mean to fight for you until you turn back from the altar. Of course, when Vega told me you were engaged to him it was a shock; but you must admit I didn't let it worry me much. I told you as soon as I saw you that I loved you——"

The girl was looking at him so strangely that Roddy was forced to pause.

"I beg your pardon!" he said.

The eyes of Inez were searching his closely. When she spoke her voice was cold and even.

"Then it was Colonel Vega," she said, "who told you I was engaged to him."

"Of course," said Roddy. "He told me the night we crossed from Curaçao."

Deep back in the serious, searching eyes Roddy thought that for an instant he detected a smile, mischievous and mocking; but as he leaned forward the eyes again grew grave and critical. With her head slightly on one side and with her hands clasped on her knee, Inez regarded him with curiosity.

"And that made no difference to you?" she asked.

"Why should it?" demanded Roddy. "A cat can look at a king; why may not I look at the most wonderful and lovely——"

In the same even tones of one asking an abstract question the girl interrupted him.

"But you must have known," she said, "that I would not engage myself to any man unless I loved him. Or do you think that, like the women here, I would marry as I was told?"

THE WHITE MICE

Roddy, not at all certain into what difficulties her questions were leading him, answered with caution.

"No," he replied doubtfully, "I didn't exactly think that, either."

"Then," declared the girl, "you must have thought, no matter how much I loved the man to whom I was engaged, that you could make me turn from him."

Roddy held out his hands appealingly.

"Don't put it that way!" he begged. "I've never thought I was better than any other man. I certainly never thought I was good enough for you. All I'm sure of is that no man on earth can care for you more. It's the best thing, the only big thing, that ever came into my life. And now it's the only thing left. Yesterday I thought I was rich, and I was glad because I had so much to offer you. But now that I've no money at all, now that I'm the Disinherited One, it doesn't seem to make any difference. At least, it would not to me. Because if I could make you care as I care for you, it wouldn't make any difference to you, either. No one on earth could love you more," pleaded Roddy. "I know it. I feel it. There is nothing else so true! Other men may bring other gifts, but 'Mine is the heart at your feet! He that hath more,'" he challenged, "'let him give!' All I know," he whispered fiercely, "is, that I *love* you, I *love* you, I *love* you!"

He was so moved, he felt what he said so truly, it was for him such happiness to speak, that his voice shook and, unknown to him, the tears stood in his eyes. In answer, he saw the eyes of the girl soften, her lips drew into a distracting and lovely line. Swiftly, with an ineffable and gracious gesture, she stooped, and catching up one of his hands held it for an instant against her cheek, and then, springing to her feet, ran from him up the garden path to the house.

Astounded, jubilant, in utter disbelief of his own senses, Roddy sat motionless. In dumb gratitude he gazed about him at the beautiful sunlit garden, drinking in deep drafts of happiness.

So sure was he that in his present state of mind he could not again, before the others, face Inez, that, like one in a dream, he stumbled through the garden to the gate that opened on the street and so returned home.

. . . .

That night McKildrick gave him permission to enter the tunnel. The gases had evaporated, and into the entrance the salt air of the sea and the tropical sun had fought their way. The party consisted of McKildrick, Peter and Roddy and, as the personal representative of Inez, Pedro, who arrived on foot from the direction of the town.

"She, herself," he confided secretly to Roddy, "wished to come."

"She did!" exclaimed Roddy joyfully. "Why didn't she?"

"I told her your mind would be filled with more important matters," returned Pedro, seeking approval. "Was I not right?"

Roddy, whose mind was filled only with Inez and who still felt the touch of her hand upon his, assented without enthusiasm.

McKildrick was for deciding by lot who should explore the underground passage, but Roddy protested that that duty belonged to him alone. With a rope around his waist, upon which he was to pull if he needed aid, an electric torch and a revolver he entered the tunnel. It led down and straight before him. The air was damp and chilly, but in breathing he now found no difficulty. Nor, at first, was his path in any way impeded. His torch showed him solid walls, white and discolored, and in places dripping with water. But of the bats, ghosts and vampires, for which Peter had cheerfully prepared him, there was no sign. Instead, the only sounds that greeted his ears were the reverberating echoes of his own footsteps. He could not tell how far he had come, but the rope he dragged behind him was each moment growing more irksome, and from this he judged he must be far advanced.

The tunnel now began to twist and turn sharply, and at one place he found a shaft for light and ventilation that had once opened to the sky. This had been closed with a gridiron of bars, upon which rested loose stones roughly held together by cement. Some of these had fallen through the bars and blocked his progress, and to advance it was necessary to remove them. He stuck his torch in a crevice and untied the rope. When he had cleared his way he left the rope where he had dropped it. Freed of this impediment he was able to proceed more quickly, and he soon found himself in that part of the tunnel that had been cut through the solid rock and which he knew lay under the waters of the harbor. The air here was less pure. His eyes began to smart and his ears to suffer from the pressure. He knew he should turn back, but until he had found the other end of the tunnel he was loath to do so. Against his better judgment he hastened his footsteps; stumbling, slipping, at times splashing in pools of water, he now ran forward. He knew that he was losing strength, and that to regain the mouth of the tunnel he would need all that was left to him. But he still pushed forward. The air had now turned foul; his head and chest ached, as when he had been long under water, and his legs were like lead. He was just upon the point of abandoning his purpose when there rose before him a solid wall. He staggered to it, and, leaning against it, joyfully beat upon it with his fists. He knew that at last only a few feet separated him from the man he had set out to save. So great was his delight and so anxious was he that Rojas should share in it, that without considering that no slight sound could penetrate the barrier, he struck three times upon it with the butt of his revolver, and then, choking and gasping like a drowning man, staggered back toward the opening. Half-way he was met by McKildrick and Peter, who, finding no pressure on the end of the rope, had drawn it to them and, fearing for Roddy's safety, had come to his rescue. They gave him an arm each, and the fresh air soon revived him. He told McKildrick what he had seen, and from his description of the second wall the engineer described how it should be opened.

"But without a confederate on the other side," he said, "we can do nothing."

"Then," declared Roddy, "the time has

come to enroll Vicenti in the Honorable Order of the White Mice."

On their return to Roddy's house they sent for Vicenti, and Roddy, having first forced him to subscribe to terrifying oaths, told the secret of the tunnel.

Tears of genuine happiness came to the eyes of the amazed and delighted Venezuelan. In his excitement he embraced Roddy and protested that with such companions and in such a cause he would gladly give his life. McKildrick assured him that when he learned of the part he was to play in the rescue he would see that they had already taken the liberty of accepting that sacrifice. It was necessary, he explained, that the wall between the tunnel and the cell should fall at the first blow. An attempt to slowly undermine it, or to pick it to pieces, would be overheard and lead to discovery. He therefore intended to rend the barrier apart by a single shock of dynamite. But in this also there was danger; not to those in the tunnel, who, knowing at what moment the mine was timed to explode, could retreat to a safe distance, but to the man they wished to set free. The problem, as McKildrick pointed it out, was to make the charges of dynamite sufficiently strong to force a breach in the wall through which Rojas could escape into the tunnel, and yet not so strong as to throw the wall upon Rojas and any one who might be with him.

"And I," cried Vicenti, "will be the one who will be with him!"

"Good!" said Roddy. "That's what we hoped. It will be your part, then, to prepare General Rojas, to keep him away from the wall when we blow it open, and to pass him through the breach to us. Everything will have to be arranged beforehand. We can't signal through the wall or they would hear it. We can only agree in advance as to the exact moment it is to fall, and then trust that nothing will hang fire, either on your side of the barrier or on ours."

"And after we get him into the tunnel!" warned Vicenti, as excited as though the fact were already accomplished, "we must still fight for his life. The explosion will bring every soldier in the fortress to the cell, and they will follow us."

"There's several sharp turns in the tunnel," said McKildrick, "and behind one of them a man with a revolver could hold back the lot!"

"I speak to do that!" cried Roddy jealously. "I speak to be Horatius!"

"'And I will stand on thy right hand,'" declared Peter; "'and hold the bridge with thee.' But you know, Roddy," he added earnestly, "you're an awful bad shot. If you go shooting up that subway in the dark you'll kill both of us. You'd better take a base-ball bat and swat them as they come round the turn."

"And then," cried Roddy, springing to his feet, "we'll rush Rojas down to the launch! And in twelve hours we'll land him safe in Curaçao. Heavens!" he exclaimed, "what a reception they'll give him!"

The cold and acid tones of McKildrick cast a sudden chill upon the enthusiasm.

"Before we design the triumphal arches," he said, "suppose we first get him out of prison."

When at last the conference came to an end and Vicenti rose to go, Roddy declared himself too excited to sleep and volunteered to accompany the doctor to his door. But the cause of his insomnia was not General Rojas but the daughter of General Rojas, and what called him forth into the moonlit Alameda was his need to think undisturbed of Inez, and, before he slept, to wish "good-night" to the house that sheltered her. In this vigil Roddy found a deep and melancholy satisfaction. From where he sat on a stone bench in the black shadows of the trees that arched the Alameda, Miramar, on the opposite side of the street, rose before him. Its yellow walls now were white and ghostlike. In the moonlight it glistened like a palace of frosted silver. The palace was asleep, and in the garden not a leaf stirred. The harbor breeze had died, and the great fronds of the palms, like rigid and glittering sword-blades, were clear-cut against the stars. The boulevard in which he sat stretched its great length, empty and silent. And Miramar seemed a dream palace set in a dream world, a world filled with strange, intangible people, intent on strange, fantastic plots. To Roddy the father, who the day before had cast him off, seemed unreal; the old man buried in a living sepulchre, and for whom in a few hours he might lose his life, was unreal; as unreal as the idea that he might lose his life. In all the little world about him there was nothing real, nothing that counted, nothing living and actual, save the girl asleep in the palace of frosted silver and his love for her.

His love for her made the fact that he was without money, and with no profession, talent or bread-and-butter knowledge that would serve to keep even himself alive, a matter of no consequence. It made the thought that Inez was promised to another man equally unimportant. The only fact was his love for her, and of that he could not doubt the outcome. He could

THE WHITE MICE

not believe God had brought into his life such happiness only to take it from him.

When he woke the next morning the necessity of seeing Inez again and at once was imperative. Since she had left him the afternoon before, in the garden of Mrs. Broughton, she had entirely occupied his thoughts. Until he saw her he could enjoy no peace. Against the circumstances that kept them apart he chafed and rebelled. He considered it would be some comfort, at least, to revisit the spot where he last had spoken with her, and where from pity or a desire to spare him she had let him tell her he loved her.

The unusual moment at which he made his call did not seem to surprise Mrs. Broughton. It was almost as though she were expecting him.

"My reason for coming at this absurd hour," began Roddy in some embarrassment, "is to apologize for running away yesterday without wishing you 'good-by.' I suddenly remembered——"

The young matron stopped him with a frown.

"I am disappointed, Roddy," she interrupted, "and hurt. If you distrust me, if you won't confide in an old friend no matter how much she may wish to help you, she can only——"

"Oh!" cried Roddy abjectly, casting aside all subterfuge, "*will* you help me? Please, Mrs. Broughton!" he begged. "*Dear* Mrs. Broughton! Fix it so I can see her. I am *so* miserable," he pleaded, "and I am so happy."

With the joyful light of the match-maker who sees her plans proceeding to success Mrs. Broughton beamed upon him.

"By a strange coincidence," she began, in tones tantalizingly slow, "a usually proud and haughty young person condescended to come to me this morning for advice. *She* doesn't distrust me. She believes——"

"And what did you advise?" begged Roddy.

"I advised her to wait in the garden until I sent a note telling you——"

Already Roddy was at the door.

"What part of the garden?" he shouted. "Never mind!" he cried in alarm, lest Mrs. Broughton should volunteer to guide him. "Don't bother to show me; I can find her."

Mrs. Broughton went into the Consulate and complained to her husband.

"It makes Roddy so selfish," she protested. "What did you think he'd do?" demanded Broughton—"ask you to go with him? You forget Roddy comes from your own happy country where no chaperon is expected to do her duty."

Inez was standing by the bench at which they

THE WHITE MICE

had parted. Above her and around her the feathery leaves of the bamboo trees whispered and shivered, shading her in a canopy of delicate sun-streaked green.

Like a man who gains the solid earth after a strenuous struggle in the waves, Roddy gave a deep sigh of content.

"It has been so hard," he said simply. "It's been so long! I have been parched, starved for a sight of you!"

At other times when they had been together the eyes of the girl always looked into his steadily or curiously. Now they were elusive, shy, glowing with a new radiance. They avoided him and smiled upon the beautiful sun-steeped garden as though sharing some hidden and happy secret.

"I sent for you," she began, "to tell you——"

Roddy shook his head emphatically.

"You didn't send for me," he said. "I came of my own accord. Last night you didn't send for me either, but all through the night I sat outside your house. This morning I am here because this is where I last saw you. And I find *you*. It's a sign! I thought my heart led me here, but I think now it was the gods! They are on my side. They fight for me. Why do you try to fight against the gods?"

THE WHITE MICE

His voice was very low, very tender. He bent forward, and the girl, still avoiding his eyes, sank back upon the bench, and Roddy, seating himself, leaned over her.

"Remember!" he whispered, "though the mills of the gods grind slow, they grind exceeding fine. The day is coming when you will never have to send for me again. You cannot escape it, or me. I am sorry—but I have come into your life—to stay!"

The girl breathed quickly, and, as though casting off the spell of his voice and the feeling it carried with it, suddenly threw out her hands and, turning quickly, faced him.

"I must tell you what makes it so hard," she said, "why I must not listen to you. It is this. I must not think of myself. I must not think of you, except—" She paused, and then added, slowly and defiantly—"as the one person who can save my father! Do you understand? Do I make it plain? I am *making use* of you. I have led you on. I have kept you near me, for his sake. I am sacrificing you—for him!" Her voice was trembling, miserable. With her clenched fist she beat upon her knee. "I had to tell you," she murmured, "I had to tell you! I had to remember," she protested fiercely, "that I am nothing, that I have no life of my own. Until he is

THE WHITE MICE

free I do not exist. I am not a girl to love, or to listen to love. I can be only the daughter of the dear, great soul who, without you, may die. And all you can be to me is the man who can save him!" She raised her eyes, unhappily, appealingly. "Even if you despised me," she whispered, "I had to tell you."

Roddy's eyes were as miserable as her own. He reached out his arms to her, as though he would shelter her from herself and from the whole world.

"But, my dear one, my wonderful one," he cried, "can't you see that's only morbid, only wicked? *You* led *me* on?" he cried. He laughed jubilantly, happily. "Did I *need* leading? Didn't I love you from the first moment you rode toward me out of the sunrise, bringing the day with you? How could I help but love you? You've done nothing to make me love you; you've only been the most glorious, the most beautiful woman——"

At a sign from the girl he stopped obediently.

"Can't I love you," he demanded, "and work for your father the more, because I love you?"

The girl sat suddenly erect and clasped her hands. Her shoulders moved slightly, as though with sudden cold.

"It frightens me!" she whispered. "Before you came I thought of him always, and nothing else, only of him. I dreamed of him; terrible, haunting dreams. Each day I prayed and worked for him. And then—" she paused, and, as though seeking help to continue, looked appealingly into Roddy's eyes. Her own were uncertain, troubled, filled with distress. "And then you came," she said. "And now I find I think of you. It is disloyal, wicked! I forget how much he suffers. I forget even how much I love him. I want only to listen to you. All the sorrow, all the misery of these last two years seems to slip from me. I find it doesn't matter, that nothing matters. I am only happy, foolishly, without reason, happy!"

In his gratitude, in his own happiness, Roddy reached out his hand. But Inez drew her own away, and with her chin resting upon it, and with her elbow on her knee, sat staring ahead of her.

"And I find this!" she whispered guiltily, like one at confession. "I find I hate to spare you for this work. Three weeks ago, when you left Curaçao, I thought a man could not risk his life in a nobler cause than the one for which you were risking yours. It seemed to me a duty—a splendid duty. But now, I am afraid —for you. I knew it first the night you swam from me across the harbor, and I followed you with my eyes, watching and waiting for you to sink and die. And I prayed for you then; and suddenly, as I prayed, I found it was not you for whom I was praying, but for myself, for my own happiness. That I wanted you to live—for me!"

The girl sprang to her feet, and Roddy rose with her, and they stood facing each other.

"Now you know," she whispered. "I had to tell you. I had to confess to you that I tried to make you care for me, hoping you would do what I wished. I did not mean to tell you that, instead, I learned to care for you. If you despise me I will understand; if you can still love me——"

"*If* I love you?" cried Roddy. "I love you so——"

For an instant, as though to shut out the look in his face, the eyes of the girl closed. She threw out her hands quickly to stop him.

"Then," she begged, "help me not to think of you. Not to think of myself. We are young. We are children. He is old: every moment counts for him. If this is the big thing in our lives we hope it is, it will last always! But with him each moment may mean the end; a horrible end, alone, among enemies, in a prison. You must give me your word—you must promise me not to tempt me to think of you. You are very generous, very strong. Help me to do this. Promise me until he is free you will not tell me you care for me, never again, until he is free. Or else"—her tone was firm, though her voice had sunk to a whisper. She drew back, and regarded him unhappily, shaking her head—"or else, I must not see you again."

There was a moment's silence, and then Roddy gave an exclamation of impatience, of protest.

"If you ask it!" he said, "I promise. How *soon* am I to see you again?"

Inez moved from him toward the house. At a little distance she stopped and regarded him in silence. Her eyes were wistful, reproachful.

"It was so hard to ask," she murmured, "and you've promised so easily!"

"How dare you!" cried Roddy. "How dare you! Easy!" He rushed on wildly, "When I want to cry out to the whole world that I love you, when I feel that every stranger sees it, when my heart beats, 'Inez, Inez, Inez,' so that I know the people in the street can hear it too. If I hadn't promised you to keep silent," he cried indignantly, "because you asked it, I'd tell you now that no other woman in all the world is loved as I love you! Easy to be silent!" he demanded, "when every drop of blood calls to you, when I breathe only when you breathe——"

"Stop!" cried the girl. For an instant she covered her face with her hands. When she lowered them her eyes were shining, radiant, laughing with happiness.

"I am so sorry!" she whispered penitently. "It was wicked. But," she pleaded, "I did so want to hear you say it just once more!"

She was very near to him. Her eyes were looking into his. What she saw in them caused her to close her own quickly. Feeling blindly with outstretched hands, she let herself sway toward him, and in an instant she was wrapped in his arms with his breathless kisses covering her lips and cheeks.

For Roddy the earth ceased revolving, he was lifted above it and heard the music of the stars. He was crowned, exalted, deified. Then the girl who had done this tore herself away and ran from him through the garden.

Neither Inez nor Roddy was in a mood to exchange polite phrases in the presence of Mrs. Broughton, and they at once separated, each in a different direction, Roddy returning to his home. There he found Sam Caldwell. He was in no better frame of mind to receive him, but Caldwell had been two hours waiting and was angry and insistent.

"At last!" he exclaimed. "I have been here since eleven. Don't tell me," he snapped, "that you've been spearing eels, because I won't believe it."

"What can I tell you," asked Roddy pleasantly, "that you will believe?"

That Caldwell had sought him out and had thought it worth his while to wait two hours for an interview seemed to Roddy to show that in the camp of his enemies matters were not moving smoothly, and that, in their opinion, he was of more interest than they cared to admit.

Caldwell began with an uneasy assumption of good-fellowship.

"I have come under a flag of truce," he said grinning. "We want to have a talk and see if we can't get together."

"Who are 'we'?" asked Roddy.

"Vega, myself, and Señora Rojas."

"Señora Rojas!" exclaimed Roddy gravely. "Are you not mistaken?"

"She sent me here," replied Caldwell. "These are my credentials." With a flourish and a bow of marked ceremony, he handed Roddy a letter.

It came from Miramar, and briefly requested that Mr. Forrester would do the Señora Rojas the honor to immediately call upon her.

Roddy caught up his hat. The prospect of a visit to the home of Inez enchanted him, and he was as greatly puzzled as to what such a visit might bring forth.

"We will go at once!" he said.

But Caldwell hung back.

"I'd rather explain it first," he said.

Already Roddy resented the fact that Caldwell was serving as the ambassador of Madame Rojas, and there was, besides, in his manner something which showed that in that service he was neither zealous nor loyal.

"Possibly Señora Rojas can do that herself," said Roddy.

"No, she can't!" returned Caldwell sharply, "because she doesn't know, and we don't mean to tell her. But I am going to tell *you*."

"Better not!" warned Roddy.

"I'll take the chance," said Caldwell. His manner was conciliating, propitiatory. "I'll take the chance," he protested, "that when you learn the truth you won't round on your own father. It isn't natural, it isn't human!"

"Caldwell on the Human Emotions!" exclaimed Roddy, grinning.

But Caldwell was too truly in earnest to be interrupted.

"Your father's spending two millions to make Vega President," he went on rapidly. "We've got to have him. We need him in our business. *You* think Rojas would make a better President. Maybe he would. But not for us. He's too old-fashioned. He's——"

"Too honest?" suggested Roddy.

"Too honest," assented Caldwell promptly. "And there's another slight objection to him. He's in jail. And you," Caldwell cried, raising his finger and shaking it in Roddy's face, "can't get him out. We can't take San Carlos, and neither can you. They have guns there that in twenty minutes could smash this town into a dust-heap. So you see, what you hope to do is impossible, absurd! Now," he urged eagerly, "why don't you give up butting your head into a stone wall, and help your father and me?"

He stopped, and in evident anxiety waited for the other to speak, but Roddy only regarded him steadily. After a pause Roddy said: "*I'm* not talking. You're the one that's talking. And," he added, "you're talking too much, too!"

"I'll risk it!" cried Caldwell stoutly. "I've never gone after a man of sense yet that I couldn't make him see things my way. Now, Señora Rojas," he went on, "only wants one thing. She wants to get her husband out of prison. She thinks Vega can do that, that he means to do it, that I mean to do it. Well—we *don't*."

Roddy's eyes half closed, the lines around

his mouth grew taut, and when he spoke his voice was harsh and had sunk to a whisper.

"I tell you," he said, "you're talking too much!"

But neither in Roddy's face nor voice did Caldwell read the danger signals.

"It doesn't suit our book," he swept on, "to get him out. Until Vega is President he must stay where he is. But his wife must not know that. She believes in *us*. She thinks the Rojas crowd only interferes with us, and she is sending for you to ask you to urge the Rojas faction to give us a free hand."

"I see," said Roddy; "and while Vega is trying to be President, Rojas may die. Have you thought of that?"

"Can we help it?" protested Caldwell. "Did *we* put him in prison? We'll have trouble enough keeping ourselves out of San Carlos. Well," he demanded, "what are you going to do?"

"At present," said Roddy, "I'm going to call on Madame Rojas."

On their walk to Miramar, Caldwell found it impossible to break down Roddy's barrier of good nature. He threatened, he bullied, he held forth open bribes; but Roddy either remained silent or laughed. Caldwell began to fear that in trying to come to terms with the enemy he had made a mistake. But still he hoped that in his obstinacy Roddy was merely stupid; he believed that in treating him as a factor in affairs they had made him vainglorious, arrogant. He was sure that if he could convince him of the utter impossibility of taking San Carlos by assault he would abandon the Rojas crowd and come over to Vega. So he enlarged upon the difficulty of that enterprise, using it as his argument in chief. Roddy, in his turn, pretended he believed San Carlos would fall at the first shot, and, as he intended, persuaded Caldwell that an attack upon the prison was the fixed purpose of the Rojas faction.

Roddy, who as a sentimental burglar had so often forced his way into the grounds of Miramar, found a certain satisfaction in at last entering it by the front door, and by invitation. His coming was obviously expected, and his arrival threw the many servants into a state of considerable excitement. Escorted by the major-domo, he was led to the drawing-room where Madame Rojas was waiting to receive him. As he entered, Inez and her sister, with Vega and General Pulido and Colonel Ramon, came in from the terrace, and Caldwell followed from the hall.

With the manner of one who considered himself already a member of the household, Vega welcomed Roddy, but without cordiality, and with condescension. To Inez, although the sight of her caused him great embarrassment, Roddy made a formal bow, to which she replied with one as formal. Señora Rojas, having ordered the servants to close the doors and the windows to the terrace, asked Roddy to be seated, and then placed herself in a chair that faced his. The others grouped themselves behind her. Roddy felt as though the odds were hardly fair. With the exception of Inez, who understood that any sign she might make in his favor would do him harm, all those present were opposed to him. This fact caused Roddy to gaze about him in pleasurable excitement and smile expectantly. He failed to see how the interview could lead to any definite result. Already he had learned from Caldwell more than he had suspected, and all that he needed to know, and, as he was determined on account of her blind faith in Vega to confide nothing to Señora Rojas, he saw no outcome to the visit as important as that it had so soon brought him again into the presence of Inez.

"Mr. Forrester," began Señora Rojas, "I have asked you to call on me to-day at the suggestion of these gentlemen. They believe that where they might fail, an appeal from me would be effective. I am going to speak to you quite frankly and openly; but when you remember I am pleading for the life of my husband you will not take offense. With no doubt the best of motives, you have allied yourself with what is known as the Rojas faction. Its object is to overthrow the President and to place my husband at Miraflores. To me, the wife of General Rojas, such an undertaking is intolerable. All I desire, all I am sure he desires, is his freedom. There are those, powerful and well equipped, who can secure it. They do not belong to the so-called Rojas faction. You, we understand, have much influence in its councils. We know that to carry out its plans you have quarrelled with your father, resigned from his company. If I venture to refer to your private affairs, it is only because I understand you yourself have spoken of them publicly, and because they show me that in your allegiance, in your mistaken allegiance to my husband, you are in earnest. But, in spite of your wish to serve him, I have asked you here to-day to beg you and your friends to relinquish your purpose. His wife and his children feel that the safety of General Rojas is in other hands, in the hands of those who have his fullest confidence and mine." In her distress, Señora Rojas leaned forward. "I beg of you,"

THE WHITE MICE

she exclaimed, "do as I ask. Leave my husband to me and to his friends. What you would do can only interfere with them. And it may lead directly to his death."

She paused, and, with her eyes fixed eagerly on Roddy's face, waited for his answer. The men standing in a group behind her nodded approvingly. Then they also turned to Roddy and regarded him sternly, as though challenging him to resist such an appeal. Roddy found his position one of extreme embarrassment. He now saw why Señora Rojas had received him in the presence of so large an audience. It was to render a refusal to grant her request the more difficult. In the group drawn up before him he saw that each represented a certain interest, each held a distinctive value. The two daughters were intended to remind him that it was against a united family he was acting; Caldwell was to recall to him that he was opposing the wishes of his father, and Vega and the two officers naturally suggested to whom Señora Rojas referred when she said her interests were in the hands of powerful and well-equipped friends. Should he tell the truth and say that of the plans of the Rojas faction he knew little or nothing, Roddy was sure he would not be believed. He was equally certain that if, in private, he confided his own plan to

Señora Rojas and told her that within the next forty-eight hours she might hope to see her husband, she would at once acquaint Vega and Caldwell with that fact. And, after the confidence made him by Caldwell, what he and Vega might not do to keep Rojas off the boards, he did not care to think. He certainly did not deem it safe to test their loyalty. He, therefore, determined that as it was impossible to tell his opponents the truth, he had better let them continue to believe he was a leader in the Rojas party, and that, with it, his only purpose was an open attack upon the fortress.

"I need not say," protested Roddy gravely, "that I am greatly flattered by your confidence. It makes me very sorry that I cannot be equally frank. But I am only a very unimportant member of the great organization that has for its leader General Rojas——"

"And I," interrupted Señora Rojas, "am the wife of that leader. Are my wishes of no weight?"

"I fear, madame," begged Roddy, in deprecatory tones, "that to millions of Venezuelans General Rojas is considered less as the husband than as the only man who can free this country from the hands of a tyrant."

At this further sign of what seemed fatuous obstinacy, Señora Rojas lost patience.

THE WHITE MICE

"A tyrant!" she exclaimed quickly. "I must protest, Mr. Forrester, that the word comes strangely from one who has denounced my husband as a traitor."

The attack confused Roddy, and to add to his discomfort it was greeted by the men in the rear of Señora Rojas with a chorus of approving exclamations. Roddy raised his eyes and regarded them gravely. In a tone of stern rebuke Señora Rojas continued:

"We have been frank and honest," she said, "but when we cannot tell whether the one with whom we treat runs with the hare or the hounds, it is difficult."

Again from the men came the murmur of approval, and Roddy, still regarding them, to prevent himself from speaking, pressed his lips tightly together.

Knowing how near Señora Rojas might be to attaining the one thing she most desired, his regret at her distress was genuine, and that, in her ignorance, she should find him a most objectionable young man he could well understand. The fact aroused in him no resentment. But to his secret amusement he found that the thought uppermost in his mind was one of congratulation that Inez Rojas was more the child of her Venezuelan father than of her American mother. Even while he deeply sympathized with Señora Rojas, viewed as a future mother-in-law, she filled him with trepidation. But from any point he could see no health in continuing the scene, and he rose and bowed.

"I am sorry," he said, "but I cannot find that any good can come of this. I assure you, you are mistaken in thinking I am of any importance, or that I carry any weight with the Rojas party. Believe me, I do not. I am doing nothing," he protested gently, "that can bring harm to your husband. No one outside of your own family can wish more sincerely for his safety."

The chorus of men interrupted him with an incredulous laugh and murmurs of disbelief.

Roddy turned upon them sharply.

"We can dispense with the claque," he said.

"My interview is with Madame Rojas. If you gentlemen have anything to discuss with me later you will come out of it much better if that lady is not present. If you don't know what I mean," he added significantly, "Caldwell can tell you."

Señora Rojas had no interest in any annoyance Roddy might feel toward her guests. She recognized only that he was leaving her. She made a final appeal. Rising to her feet, she exclaimed indignantly:

"I refuse to believe that against the wishes

THE WHITE MICE

of myself and my family you will persist in this. It is incredible! I can no longer be content only to ask you not to interfere—I forbid it."

She advanced toward him, her eyes flashing with angry tears. Roddy, in his sympathy with her distress, would have been glad, with a word, to end it, but he felt he could not trust to her discretion. Her next speech showed him that his instinct was correct. Accepting his silence as a refusal, she turned with an exclamation to Pino Vega.

"If you will not listen to a woman," she protested, "you may listen to a man." With a gesture she signified Vega. He stepped eagerly forward.

"I am at your service," he said.

"Speak to him," Señora Rojas commanded. "Tell him! Forbid him to continue."

Roddy received the introduction of Vega into the scene with mixed feelings. To the best of his ability he was trying to avoid a quarrel, and in his fuller knowledge of the situation he knew that for Señora Rojas it would be best if she had followed his wishes, and had brought the interview to an end. That Vega, who was planning treachery to Rojas, should confront him as the champion of Rojas, stirred all the combativeness in Roddy that he was endeavoring to subdue. When Vega turned to him he welcomed that gentleman with a frown.

"As the son of this house," Vega began dramatically, "as the representative, in his absence, of General Rojas, I forbid you to meddle further in this affair."

The demand was unfortunately worded. A smile came to Roddy's eyes, and the color in his cheeks deepened. He turned inquiringly to Señora Rojas.

"The son of this house," he repeated. "The gentleman expresses himself awkwardly. What does he mean?"

Since Inez had entered the room Roddy had not once permitted himself to look toward her. Now he heard from where she stood a quick movement and an exclamation.

For an instant, a chill of doubt held him silent. Within the very hour, she had told him that to keep him loyal to her father she had traded on his interest in her. Had she, for the same purpose and in the same way, encouraged Vega? To Roddy, she had confessed what she had done, and that she loved him. With that he was grandly content. But was she still hoping by her promise of marriage to Vega to hold him in allegiance, not to herself, but to her father? Was her exclamation one of warning? Had he, by his question, precipitated some explanation that Inez wished to avoid? He cast toward her a glance of anxious inquiry. To his relief, Inez reassured him with a nod, and a smile of trust and understanding.

The exchange of glances was lost neither upon Vega nor upon Señora Rojas. In turn, they looked at each other, their eyes filled with angry suspicion.

What she had witnessed caused Señora Rojas to speak with added asperity.

"Colonel Vega has my authority for what he says," she exclaimed. "He *is* the son of this house. He is the future husband of my daughter Inez."

The exclamation that now came from Inez was one of such surprise and protest that every one turned toward her.

The girl pushed from her the chair on which she had been leaning and walked toward her mother. Her eyes were flashing, but her manner was courteous and contained.

"Why do you say that?" she asked quietly. "Has Colonel Vega told you that, as he has told others? Because it is not true!"

Señora Rojas, amazed and indignant, stared at her daughter as though she doubted she had heard her.

"Inez!" she exclaimed.

"It must be set right," said the girl.

THE WHITE MICE

"Colonel Vega presumes too far on the services he has shown my father. I am not going to marry him. I have told him so repeatedly. He is deceiving you in this, as he is deceiving you in matters more important. He is neither the son of this house nor the friend of this house. And it is time that he understood that we know it!"

In her distress, Señora Rojas turned instinctively to Vega.

"Pino!" she exclaimed. "You *told* me! You told me it was her secret, that she wished to keep it even from her mother, but that you thought it your duty to tell me. Why?" she demanded. "Why?"

Vega, his eyes flaming, in a rage of mortification and wounded vanity threw out his arms.

"My dear lady!" he cried, "it was because I hoped! I still hope," he protested. "Inez has been poisoned by this man!" He pointed with a shaking finger at Roddy. "He has filled her mind with tales against me." He turned to Inez. "Is it not true?" he challenged.

Inez regarded him coldly, disdainfully.

"No, it is not true," she said. "It is the last thing he would do. Because, until this moment, Mr. Forrester thought that what you told him was a fact." She raised her voice. "And he is incapable of speaking ill of a man—"

THE WHITE MICE

she hesitated, and then, smiling slightly as though in enjoyment of the mischief she was making, added, "he knew was his unsuccessful rival."

Furious, with a triumphant exclamation, Vega turned to Señora Rojas.

"You hear!" he cried. "My rival!"

Inez moved quickly toward Roddy. Placing herself at his side, she faced the others.

Her eyes were wide with excitement, with fear at what she was about to do. As though begging permission, she raised them to Roddy and, timidly stretching out her hand, touched his arm. "Mother," she said, "I am going to marry Mr. Forrester!"

VIII

The silence that greeted the announcement of Inez was broken in a startling fashion. Before her mother could recover from her amazement one of the windows to the garden was thrown open, and a man burst through it sprang toward Vega. He was dishevelled, and breathless; from a wound in his forehead a line of blood ran down his cheek. His appearance was so alarming that all of those who, the instant before, had been staring in astonishment at Inez now turned to the intruder. They recognized him as the personal servant of Vega. Without considering the presence of the others, the valet spoke as he crossed the room.

"The police are in your house," he panted. "They have searched it; taken the papers. They tried to stop me." He drew his hand across his face and showed it streaked with blood. "But I escaped by the harbor. The boat is at the wharf. You have not a moment!" His eyes wandered toward Pulido and Ramon, and he exclaimed delightedly, "You also!" he cried; "there is still time!"

General Pulido ran to the window.

THE WHITE MICE

"There is still time!" he echoed. "By the boat we can reach Quinta Tortola at the appointed hour. Colonel Ramon," he commanded, "remain with Señor Caldwell. You, Pino, come with me!"

But Vega strode furiously toward Roddy.

"No!" he shouted. "This man first! My honor first!"

At this crisis of his fortunes, Sam Caldwell, much to the surprise of Roddy, showed himself capable of abrupt action. He threw his arm around the waist of Vega, and ran him to the window.

"Damn your honor!" he shrieked. "You take your orders from *me!* Go to the meeting-place!"

Struggling, not only in the arms of Caldwell but in those of Pulido and the valet, Vega was borne to the terrace. As he was pushed from the window he stretched out his arm toward Roddy.

"When we meet again," he cried, "I kill you!"

Roddy looked after him with regret. More alarming to him than the prospect of a duel was the prospect of facing Señora Rojas. For the moment Vega and his personal danger had averted the wrath that Roddy knew was still to come, but with the departure of Vega he saw

THE WHITE MICE

it could no longer be postponed. He turned humbly to Señora Rojas. The scene through which that lady had just passed had left her trembling; but the sight of Roddy confronting her seemed at once to restore her self-possession. Anxiously, but in a tone of deep respect, Roddy addressed her:

"I have the great honor," he said, "to inform——"

After one indignant glance Señora Rojas turned from him to her daughter. Her words sounded like the dripping of icicles.

"You will leave the room," she said. She again glanced at Roddy. "You will leave the house."

Not since when, as a child, he had been sent to stand in a corner had Roddy felt so guilty. And to his horror he found he was torn with a hysterical desire to laugh.

"But, Madame Rojas," he protested hastily, "it is impossible for me to leave until I make clear to you——"

In the fashion of the country, Señora Rojas clapped her hands.

"Surely," she exclaimed, "you will not subject me to a scene before the servants."

In answer to her summons the doors flew open, and the frightened servants, who had heard of the blood-stained messenger, pushed into the room. With the air of a great lady dismissing an honored guest Señora Rojas bowed to Roddy, and Roddy, accepting the inevitable, bowed deeply in return.

As he walked to the door he cast toward Inez an unhappy look of apology and appeal. But the smile with which she answered seemed to show that, to her, their discomfiture was in no way tragic. Roddy at once took heart and beamed with gratitude. In the look he gave her he endeavored to convey his assurance of the devotion of a lifetime.

"Good-by," said Inez pleasantly.

"Good-by," said Roddy.

On coming to Porto Cabello Sam Caldwell had made his headquarters at the home of the United States Consul, who owed his appointment to the influence of Mr. Forrester, and who, in behalf of that gentleman, was very justly suspected by Alvarez of "pernicious activity." On taking his leave of Señora Rojas, which he did as soon as Roddy had been shown the door, Caldwell hastened to the Consulate, and, as there might be domiciliary visits to the houses of all the Vegaistas, Colonel Ramon, seeking protection as a political refugee, accompanied him.

The police had precipitated the departure of

Vega from the city by only a few hours. He had planned to leave it and to join his adherents in the mountains that same afternoon, and it was only to learn the result of the final appeal to Roddy that he had waited. As they hastened through the back streets to the Consulate, Ramon said:

"It was not worth waiting for. Young Forrester told nothing. And why? Because he knows nothing!"

"To me," growled Caldwell, "he makes a noise like a joker in the pack. I don't mind telling you he's got me listening. He wouldn't have thrown up his job and quarrelled with his father and Señora Rojas if he wasn't pretty sure he was in right. Vega tells me, three weeks ago Roddy went to Curaçao to ask Madame Rojas to help him get her husband out of prison. Instead, she turned him down *hard*. But did that phase him? No! I believe he's still working—working at this moment on some plan of his own to get Rojas free. Every night he goes out in his launch with young De Peyster. Where do they go? They *say* they go fishing. Well, maybe! We can't follow them, for they douse the lights and their motor is too fast for us. But, to me, it looks like a rescue, for the only way they could rescue Rojas would be from the harbor.

If they have slipped him tools and he is cutting his way to the water, some dark night they'll carry him off in that damned launch. And then," he exclaimed angrily, "where would I be? That old Rip Van Winkle has only got to show his face, and it would be all over but the shouting. He'd lose us what we've staked on Vega, and he'd make us carry out some of the terms of our concession that would cost us a million more."

Ramon exclaimed with contempt.

"Forrester!" he cried. "He is only a boy!"

"Any boy," snapped Caldwell, impatiently, "who is clever enough to get himself engaged to the richest girl in Venezuela, under the guns of her mother and Pino Vega, is old enough to vote. I take my hat off to him."

The Venezuelan turned his head and looked meaningly at Caldwell; his eyes were hard and cruel.

"I regret," he said, "but he must be stopped."

"No, you don't!" growled Caldwell; "that's not the answer. We won't stop *him*. We'll let *him* go! It's the other man we'll stop—Rojas!"

"Yes, yes!" returned Ramon eagerly. "That is the only way left. Rojas must die!"

"Die!" laughed Caldwell comfortably. "Not a bit like it! I'm rather planning to improve his health." He stopped and glanced up and down the narrow street. It was empty. He laid his hand impressively on the arm of the Venezuelan.

"To-day," he whispered, "some one will send a letter—an anonymous letter—to San Carlos, telling the Commandante why General Rojas would be more comfortable in another cell."

. . . .

From Miramar, Roddy returned directly to his house. On the way he found the city in a ferment; all shops had closed, the plazas and cafés were crowded, and the Alameda was lined with soldiers. Wherever a few men gathered together the police ordered them to separate; and in the driveways, troopers of Alvarez, alert and watchful, each with his carbine on his hip, rode slowly at a walk, glancing from left to right. At his house, Roddy found gathered there all of the White Mice: Peter, McKildrick, Vicenti, and Pedro. They had assembled, he supposed, to learn the result of his visit to Miramar, but they were concerned with news more important. Vicenti had called them together to tell them that, at any moment, the Rojas faction might rise and attempt to seize the city and San Carlos. The escape of

THE WHITE MICE

Vega, and the fact, which was now made public, that he had proclaimed himself in revolt, had given the Rojas faction the opportunity for which it had been waiting. The city was denuded of Government troops. For hours they had been pouring out of it in pursuit of Vega and his little band of revolutionists; and until reinforcements should arrive from Caracas, which might not be in twenty-four hours, the city was defenseless. The moment for the Rojas party had come.

But Vicenti feared that the assault on San Carlos would result, not only in the death of many of those who attacked it, but also would be the signal on the inside for the instant assassination of Rojas. It therefore was imperative, before the attack was made, to get Rojas out of prison. He dared not inform even the leaders of the Rojas party of the proposed rescue. It must be attempted only by those who could be absolutely trusted, those already in the secret. And it was for that purpose he had called the White Mice together. When Roddy arrived they had, subject to his approval, arranged their plan. From what Vicenti had learned, the assault on the fortress would be made at midnight. It was accordingly agreed that at nine o'clock, when it would be quite dark, they would blow open the wall. Roddy,

McKildrick, and Peter would dine together at Roddy's house, and at eight, in the launch, would leave his wharf. Pedro, whose presence would assure General Rojas of the good intentions of the others, was directed to so arrange his departure from Miramar as to arrive by the shore route at the wharf in time to accompany them. And Vicenti, who had set his watch with McKildrick's, was at once to inform General Rojas of what was expected to happen, and at nine o'clock, when the wall fell, to rush with him through the breach.

In the *patio* the men, standing and in silence, drank to the success of their undertaking, and then, after each had shaken hands with the others, separated. By Roddy's orders Pedro was to inform Inez of their plan and to tell her that, if the Rojas party, in its attack upon the city, was successful, her father might that night sleep at Miramar. If, after his release, the issue were still in doubt, the launch would carry him to Curaçao.

Vicenti left for San Carlos. In case it should be necessary to make the dash to Willemstad, Peter remained at the house to collect for the voyage provisions, medicine, stimulants, casks of water, and McKildrick and Roddy departed in the launch to lay the mine which was to destroy the barrier. On their way they stopped

THE WHITE MICE

at the light-house, where McKildrick collected what he wanted for that purpose. It was now four o'clock in the afternoon, and by five they had entered the tunnel and reached the wall. McKildrick dug a hole in the cement a few feet above the base, and in this shoved a stick of dynamite of sixty per cent. nitro, and attached a number six cap and a fuse a foot long. This would burn for one minute and allow whoever lighted it that length of time to get under cover. In case of a miss-fire, he had brought with him extra sticks, fuses, and caps. These, with drills and a sledge-hammer, they hid in a corner of the wall.

In the damp darkness of the tunnel it was difficult to believe that outside the sun was still shining.

"If it were only night!" said Roddy. "I hate to leave it. I'd only have to touch a match to that, and he'd be free."

"Free of the cell," assented McKildrick, "but we could never get him away. The noise will bring the whole garrison. It will be like heaving a brick into a hornets' nest. We must wait for darkness. This is no matinée performance."

On the return trip to the city they sat in silence, the mind of each occupied by his own thoughts. How serious these thoughts were

THE WHITE MICE

neither cared to confess in words, but as they passed under the guns of the fortress they glanced at each other and smiled.

"You mustn't think, Mac," said Roddy gratefully, "I don't appreciate what you're doing. You stand to lose a lot!"

"I can always get another job," returned McKildrick.

"You can't if one of these fellows puts a bullet in you," said Roddy. "You know you are making a big sacrifice, and I thank you for it."

McKildrick looked at him in some embarrassment.

"You stand to lose more than any of us," he said. "I'm told you are to be congratulated." His eyes were so full of sympathy and good feeling that Roddy held out his hand.

"You're the first one to do it," he said happily; "and it's good to hear. Mac!" he exclaimed, in awe-struck tones, "I'm the happiest, luckiest, and the least deserving beggar in all the world!"

McKildrick smiled dryly.

"I seem to have heard something like that before," he said.

"Never!" cried Roddy stoutly. "Other poor devils may have thought so, but I *know*. It never happened to any one but me!"

McKildrick turned his eyes seaward and frowned.

"I even used the same lines myself once," he said; "but I found I'd got hold of some other fellow's part. So if anything *should* come my way to-night it wouldn't make such a lot of difference."

Roddy took one hand from the wheel and, leaning forward, touched McKildrick on the knee.

"I'm sorry," he said; "I didn't know."

McKildrick nodded, and as though glad of an interruption, held up his hand.

"Listen!" he cried. "Stop the engine!"

Roddy let the launch slip forward on her own headway. In the silence that followed they heard from the city the confused murmur of a mob and the sharp bark of pistols. They looked at each other significantly.

"The surface indications seem to show," said McKildrick, "that things are loosening up. I guess it's going to be one of those nights!"

As they rounded the point and the whole of the harbor front came into view, they saw that the doors of the bonded warehouses had been broken open, and that the boxes and bales they contained had been tumbled out upon the wharf and piled into barricades. From behind these, and from the windows of the custom-house, men not in uniform, and evidently of the Rojas faction, were firing upon the tiny gunboat in the harbor, and from it their rifle-fire was being answered by an automatic gun. With full speed ahead, Roddy ran the gauntlet of this cross-fire, and in safety tied up to his own wharf.

"Go inside," he commanded, "and find out what has happened. And tell Peter we'll take his cargo on board now. Until we're ready to start I'll stay by the launch and see no one tries to borrow her."

Peter and McKildrick returned at once, and with gasoline, tins of biscuit and meat, and a cask of drinking water, stocked the boat for her possible run to Curaçao. The Rojas party, so Peter informed them, had taken the barracks in the suburbs and, preliminary to an attack on the fortress, had seized the custom-house which faced it; but the artillery barracks, which were inside the city, were still in the hands of the government troops. Until they were taken, with the guns in them, the Rojas faction were without artillery, and against the fortress could do nothing. It was already dusk, and, in half an hour, would be night. It was for this the Rojas crowd were waiting. As yet, of Vega and his followers no news had reached the city. But the government troops

THE WHITE MICE

were pursuing him closely, and it was probable that an engagement had already taken place.

"By this time," said Roddy, "Vicenti has told Rojas, and in an hour Pedro will arrive, and then we start. Go get something to eat, and send my dinner out here. I've some tinkering to do on the engine."

Before separating, McKildrick suggested that Peter and Roddy should set their watches by his, which was already set to agree with Vicenti's.

"For, should anything happen to me," he explained, "you boys must blow up the wall, and you must know just when you are to do it. Roddy knows *how* to do it, and," he added to Peter, "I'll explain it to you while we're at dinner."

They left Roddy on his knees, busily plying his oil-can, and crossed the garden. In the *patio* they found the table ready for dinner, and two lamps casting a cheerful light upon the white cloth and flashing from the bottle of red Rioja.

As they seated themselves, one of the stray bullets that were singing above the housetops dislodged a tile, and the pieces of red clay fell clattering into the courtyard. Peter reached for the claret and, with ostentatious slowness, filled McKildrick's glass.

THE WHITE MICE

"Dynasties may come," he said, "and dynasties may go; but I find one always dines."

"Why not?" replied McKildrick. "Napoleon said an army is a collection of stomachs. Why should you and I pretend to be better soldiers than Napoleon's?"

As a signal to the kitchen he clapped his hands; but the servant who answered came not from the kitchen, but from the street. His yellow skin was pale with fright. He gasped and pointed into the shadow at a soldier who followed him. The man wore the uniform of a hospital steward and on his arm the badge of the Red Cross. He stepped forward and, glancing with concern from Peter to McKildrick, saluted mechanically.

"Doctor Vicenti!" he exclaimed; "he wishes to see you. He is outside on a stretcher. We are taking him to the hospital, but he made us bring him here first." The man shook his head sharply. "He is dying!" he said.

In this sudden threat of disaster to their plan the thought of both the conspirators was first for Rojas.

"My God!" cried Peter, and stared helplessly at the older man.

"Dying?" protested McKildrick. "I saw him an hour ago; he was——"

"He was caring for the wounded in the

streets. He was shot," answered the man gravely, laying his finger on his heart, "here!"

"Caring for the wounded!" cried McKildrick. "Why in hell wasn't he——"

"Be quiet!" warned Peter.

McKildrick checked himself and, followed by Peter, ran to the street. In the light from the open door he saw an army stretcher, and on it a figure of a man covered with a blanket. An officer and the soldiers who had borne the stretcher stood in the shadow. With an exclamation of remorse and sympathy, McKildrick advanced quickly and leaned forward. But the man on the stretcher was not Vicenti. To make sure, McKildrick bent lower, and in an instant the stranger threw out his arms and, clasping him around the neck, dragged him down. At the same moment the stretcher bearers fell upon him from the rear, and, wrenching back his arms, held them together until the officer clasped his wrists with handcuffs. From Peter he heard a muffled roar and, twisting his head, saw him rolling on the sidewalk. On top of him were a half-dozen soldiers; when they lifted him to his feet his wrists also were in manacles.

McKildrick's outbursts were silenced by the officer.

"You need not tell me you are Americans,"

he said, "and if you go quietly no harm will come. We wish only to keep you out of mischief."

"Go?" demanded Peter. "Go where?"

"To the *cartel*," said the officer, smiling. "You will be safer there."

He stepped into the light and waved his sword, and from across the street came running many more soldiers. A squad of these the officer detailed to surround his prisoners. To the others he said: "Search the house. Find the third one, Señor Forrester. Do not harm him, but," he added meaningly, "bring him with you!"

At the word, Peter swung his arms free from the man who held them. With a yell of warning, which he hoped would reach Roddy, and pulling impotently at his handcuffs, he dashed into the house, the soldiers racing at his heels.

Roddy had finished his inspection of his engine, but was still guarding the launch, waiting with impatience for some one to bring him his dinner. He was relieved to note that from the direction of Miramar there was no sound of fighting. In the lower part of the city he could hear a brisk fusillade, but, except from the custom-house, the firing had more the sound of street fighting than of an organized attack. From this, he judged the assault on

THE WHITE MICE

the artillery barracks had not yet begun. He flashed his electric torch on his watch, and it showed half past seven. There was still a half-hour to wait. He rose and, for the hundredth time, spun the wheel of his engine, examined his revolver, and yawned nervously. It was now quite dark. Through the trees and shrubs in the garden he could see the lights on the dinner-table and the spectacle made him the more hungry. To remind the others that he was starving, he gave a long whistle. It was at once cautiously answered, to his surprise, not from the house but from a spot a hundred feet from him, on the shore of the harbor. He decided, as it was in the direction one would take in walking from Miramar, that Pedro had arrived, and he sighed with relief. He was about to repeat his signal of distress when, from the *patio*, there arose a sudden tumult. In an instant, with a crash of broken glass and china, the lights were extinguished, and he heard the voice of Peter shrieking his name. He sprang from the launch and started toward the garden. At that moment a heavy body crashed upon the gravel walk, and there was the rush of many feet.

"Roddy!" shrieked the voice of Peter, "they're taking us to jail. They're coming after *you*. Run! Run like hell!"

THE WHITE MICE

In the darkness Roddy could see nothing. He heard what sounded like an army of men trampling and beating the bushes. His first thought was that he must attempt a rescue. He jerked out his gun and raced down the wharf. Under his flying feet the boards rattled and Peter heard him coming.

"Go back!" he shrieked furiously. "You can't help us! You've got work to do! Do it!"

The profanity with which these orders were issued convinced Roddy that Peter was very much in earnest and in no personal danger.

The next moment he was left no time for further hesitation. His flying footsteps had been heard by the soldiers as well as by Peter, and from the garden they rushed shouting to the beach. Against such odds Roddy saw that to rescue Peter was impossible, while at the same time, even alone, he still might hope to rescue Rojas.

He cast loose the painter of the launch, and with all his strength shoved it clear. He had apparently acted not a moment too soon, for a figure clad in white leaped upon the wharf and raced toward him. Roddy sprang to the wheel and the launch moved slowly in a circle. At the first sound of the revolving screw there came from the white figure a cry of dismay.

THE WHITE MICE

It was strangely weak, strangely familiar, strangely feminine.

"Roddy!" cried the voice. "It is I, Inez!"

With a shout of amazement, joy, and consternation, Roddy swung the boat back toward the shore, and by the breadth of an oar-blade cleared the wharf. There was a cry of relief, of delight, a flutter of skirts, and Inez sprang into it. In an agony of fear for her safety, Roddy pushed her to the bottom of the launch.

"Get down!" he commanded. "They can see your dress. They'll fire on you."

From the shore an excited voice cried in Spanish: "Do I shoot, sergeant?"

"No!" answered another. "Remember your orders!"

"But he escapes!" returned the first voice, and on the word there was a flash, a report, and a bullet whined above them. Another and others followed, but the busy chug-chug of the engine continued undismayed and, as the noise of its progress died away, the firing ceased. Roddy left the wheel, and, stooping, took Inez in his arms. Behind them the city was a blaze of light, and the sky above it was painted crimson. From the fortress, rockets, hissing and roaring, signalled to the barracks; from the gun-boat, the quick-firing guns were stabbing the darkness with swift, vindictive flashes.

THE WHITE MICE

In different parts of the city incendiary fires had started and were burning sullenly, sending up into the still night air great, twisting columns of sparks. The rattle of musketry was incessant.

With his arm about her and her face pressed to his, Inez watched the spectacle unseeingly. For the moment it possessed no significance. And for Roddy, as he held her close, it seemed that she must feel his heart beating with happiness. He had never dared to hope that such a time would come, when they would be alone together, when it would be his right to protect and guard her, when, again and again, he might try to tell her how he loved her. Like one coming from a dream, Inez stirred and drew away.

"Where are we going?" she whispered.

"We're going to the tunnel to save your father," answered Roddy.

The girl gave a little sigh of content and again sank back into the shelter of his arm.

They passed the fortress, giving it a wide berth, and turned in toward the shore. The city now lay far to the right, and the clamor of the conflict came to them but faintly.

"Tell me," said Roddy, "why did you come to the wharf?" He seemed to be speaking of something that had happened far back in the past, of a matter which he remembered as having once been of vivid importance, but which now was of consequence only that it concerned her.

Reluctantly Inez broke the silence that had enveloped them.

"They came to the house and arrested Pedro," she said. To her also the subject seemed to be of but little interest. She spoke as though it were only with an effort she could recall the details. "I knew you needed him to convince father you were friends. So, as he could not come, I came. Did I do right?"

"Whatever you do is right," answered Roddy. "We might as well start life with that proposition as a fixed fact."

"And do you want me with you now?" whispered the girl.

"Do I want you with me!" Roddy exclaimed, in mock exasperation. "Don't provoke me!" he cried. "I am trying," he protested, "to do my duty, while what I would like to do is to point this boat the other way, and elope with you to Curaçao. So, if you love your father, don't make yourself any more distractingly attractive than you are at this moment. If you don't help me to be strong I will run away with you."

Inez laughed, softly and happily, and, leaning toward him, kissed him.

"That's not helping me!" protested Roddy.

"It is for the last time," said Inez, "until my father is free."

"That may not be for months!" cried Roddy.

"It is for the last time," repeated Inez.

Roddy concealed the launch in the cove below El Morro and, taking from the locker a flask of brandy and an extra torch, led the way up the hill. When they drew near to the fortress, fearing a possible ambush, he left Inez and proceeded alone to reconnoitre. But El Morro was undisturbed, and as he and McKildrick had left it. He returned for Inez, and at the mouth of the tunnel halted and pointed to a place well suited for concealment.

"You will wait there," he commanded.

"No," returned the girl quietly, "I will go with you. You forget I am your sponsor, and," she added gently, "I am more than that. After this, where you go, I go."

As she spoke there came from the wharf of the custom-house, lying a mile below them, a flash of flame. It was followed by others, and instantly, like an echo, the guns of the fort replied.

"Shrapnel!" cried Roddy. "They've captured the artillery barracks, and we haven't a moment to lose!"

He threw himself on the levers that moved

the slabs of stone and forced them apart. Giving Inez his hand, he ran with her down the steps of the tunnel.

"But why," cried Inez, "is there more need for haste now than before?"

Roddy could not tell her the assault of the Rojas party on the fortress might lead to a reprisal in the assassination of her father.

"The sound of the cannon," he answered evasively, "will drown out what we do."

Roddy was now more familiar with the various windings of the tunnel, and they advanced quickly. Following the circles of light cast by their torches, they moved so rapidly that when they reached the wall both were panting. Roddy held his watch in front of the light and cried out with impatience.

"Ten minutes!" he exclaimed, "and every minute—" He checked himself and turned to the wall. The dynamite, with the cap and fuse attached, was as McKildrick had placed it. For a tamp he scooped up from the surface of the tunnel a handful of clay, and this he packed tightly over the cap, leaving the fuse free. He led Inez back to a safe distance from the wall, and there, with eyes fastened on Roddy's watch, they waited. The seconds dragged interminably. Neither spoke, and the silence of the tunnel weighed upon them like the silence of a grave. But even buried as they were many feet beneath the ramparts, they could hear above them the reverberations of the cannon.

"They are firing in half-minute intervals," whispered Roddy. "I will try to set off the dynamite when they fire, so that in the casements, at least, no one will hear me. When the explosion comes," he directed, "wait until I call you, and if I shout to you to run, for God's sake," he entreated, "don't delay an instant, but make for the mouth of the tunnel."

Inez answered him in a tone of deep reproach. "You are speaking," she said, "to a daughter of General Rojas." Her voice trembled, but, as Roddy knew, it trembled from excitement. "You must not think of *me*," commanded the girl. "I am here to help, not to be a burden. And," she added gently, her love speaking to him in her voice, "we leave this place together, or not at all."

Her presence had already shaken Roddy, and now her words made the necessity of leaving her seem a sacrifice too great to be required of him. Almost brusquely, he started from her.

"I must go," he whispered. "Wish me good luck for your father."

"May God preserve you both!" answered the girl.

THE WHITE MICE

As he walked away Roddy turned and shifted his light for what he knew might be his last look at her. He saw her, standing erect as a lance, her eyes flashing. Her lips were moving and upon her breast her fingers traced the sign of the cross.

Roddy waited until his watch showed a minute to nine o'clock. To meet the report of the next gun, he delayed a half-minute longer, and then lit the fuse, and, running back, flattened himself against the side of the tunnel. There was at last a dull, rumbling roar and a great crash of falling rock. Roddy raced to the sound and saw in the wall a gaping, black hole. Through it, from the other side, lights showed dimly. In the tunnel he was choked with a cloud of powdered cement. He leaped through this and, stumbling over a mass of broken stone, found himself in the cell. Except for the breach in the wall the explosion had in no way disturbed it. The furniture was in place, a book lay untouched upon the table; in the draft from the tunnel the candles flickered drunkenly. But of the man for whom he sought, for whom he was risking his life, there was no sign. With a cry of amazement and alarm Roddy ran to the iron door of the cell. It was locked and bolted. Now that the wall no longer deadened the sound his ears were assailed by all the fierce clamor of the battle. Rolling toward him down the stone corridor came the splitting roar of the siege guns, the rattle of rifle fire, the shouts of men. Against these sounds, he recognized that the noise of the explosion had carried no farther than the limits of the cell, or had been confused with the tumult overhead. He knew, therefore, that from that source he need not fear discovery. But in the light of the greater fact that his attempt at rescue had failed, his own immediate safety became of little consequence. He turned and peered more closely into each corner of the cell. The clouds of cement thrown up by the dynamite had settled; and, hidden by the table, Roddy now saw, huddled on the stone floor, with his back against the wall, the figure of a man. With a cry of relief and concern, Roddy ran toward him and flashed his torch. It was Vicenti. The face of the young doctor was bloodless, his eyes wild and staring. He raised them imploringly.

"Go!" he whispered. His voice was weak and racked with pain. "Some one has betrayed us. They know everything!"

Roddy exclaimed furiously, and, for an instant, his mind was torn with doubts.

"And you!" he demanded. "Why are you here?"

Her fingers traced the sign of the cross.

THE WHITE MICE

reading the suspicion in his eyes, [Vicenti raised his] hands; the pantomime was sufficiently eloquent. In deep circles around his [wrists] were new, raw wounds.

"They tried to make me tell," he whispered. "They think you're coming in the launch, with the others. When I wouldn't answer, they put me here. It was their jest. You were to find me instead of the other. They are waiting now on the ramparts above us, waiting for you to come in the launch. They know nothing of the tunnel."

Roddy's eyes were fixed in horror on the bleeding wrists.

"They tortured you!" he cried.

"I fainted. When I came to," whispered the doctor, "I found myself locked in here. For God's sake," he pleaded, "save yourself!"

"And Rojas?" demanded Roddy.

"That is impossible!" returned Vicenti, answering Roddy's thought. "He is in another cell, far removed, the last one, in this corridor."

"In *this* corridor!" demanded Roddy.

Vicenti feebly reached out his hand and seized Roddy's arm.

"It is impossible!" he pleaded. "You can't get out of this cell."

"I will get out of it the same way I got in," answered Roddy. "Can you walk?"

293

With his eyes, Vicenti measured t[he distance] to the breach in the wall.

"Help me!" he begged.

Roddy lifted him to his feet and, w[ith his] arm around him, supported him into the [tunnel.] From his flask he gave him brandy, and V[icenti] nodded gratefully.

"Further on," directed Roddy, "you will find Señorita Rojas. Tell her she must go at once. Don't let her know that I am going after her father."

"It is madness!" cried Vicenti. "The turnkey is in the corridor, and at any moment they may come to assassinate Rojas."

"Then I've no time to waste," exclaimed Roddy. "Get the Señorita and yourself out of the tunnel, and get out *quick!*"

"But you?" pleaded Vicenti. "You can do nothing."

"If I must," answered Roddy, "I can blow the whole damn fort to pieces!"

He ran to the spot where McKildrick had placed the extra explosives. With these and the hand-drill, the sledge, and carrying his hat filled with clay, he again climbed through the breach into the cell. The fierceness of the attack upon the fort had redoubled, and to repulse it the entire strength of the garrison had been summoned to the ramparts, leaving, so far as Roddy could see through the bars, the corridor unguarded. The door of the cell hung on three trunnions, and around the lowest hinge the weight of the iron door had loosened the lead and cement in which, many years before, it had been embedded. With his drill, Roddy increased the opening to one large enough to receive the fingers of his hand and into it welded a stick of dynamite. To this he affixed a cap and fuse, and clapping on his tamp of clay, lit the fuse, and ran into the tunnel. He had cut the fuse to half-length, and he had not long to wait. With a roar that shook the cell and echoed down the corridor, that portion of the wall on which the bars hung was torn apart, and the cell door, like a giant gridiron, fell sprawling across the corridor. Roddy could not restrain a lonely cheer. So long as the battle drowned out the noise of the explosions and called from that part of the prison all those who might oppose him, the rescue of Rojas again seemed feasible. With another charge of dynamite the last cell in the corridor could be blown open, and Rojas would be free. But Roddy was no longer allowed, undisturbed, to blast his way to success. Almost before the iron door had struck the floor of the corridor there leaped into the opening the burly figure of the turnkey. In one hand

THE WHITE MICE

he held a revolver, in the other a lantern. Lifting the lantern above his head, he stood balancing himself upon the fallen grating. Hanging to his belt, Roddy saw a bunch of keys. The sight of the keys went to his head like swift poison. For them he suddenly felt himself capable of murder. The dust hung in a cloud between the two men, and before the turnkey could prepare for the attack Roddy had flung himself on him and, twisting the bones of his wrist, had taken the revolver. With one hand on the throat of the turnkey he shoved the revolver up under his chin until the circle of steel sank into his flesh.

"Don't cry out!" whispered Roddy. "Do as I tell you, or I'll blow your head off. Take me to the cell of General Rojas!"

Brave as the man had been the moment before, the kiss of the cold muzzle turned his purpose to ice. The desire to live was all-compelling. Choking, gasping, his eyes rolling appealingly, he nodded assent. With the revolver at his back he ran down the corridor, and, as he ran, without further direction, fumbled frantically at his keys. At the end of the corridor he separated one from the others, and with a trembling hand unlocked and pushed open a cell door.

The cell was steeped in darkness. Roddy

threw the turnkey sprawling into it, and with his free hand closed his fingers over the key in the lock.

"General Rojas!" he called. "Come out! You are free!"

A shadowy figure suddenly confronted him; out of the darkness a voice, fearless and unshaken, answered.

"What do you wish with me?" demanded the voice steadily. "Is this assassination? Are you my executioner?"

"Good God, no!" cried Roddy. "Fifty-four, four! I'm the man that gave you the warning. The tunnel!" he cried. "The tunnel is open." He shoved the butt of the revolver toward the shadow. "Take this!" he commanded; "if I've lied to you, shoot me. But come!"

General Rojas stepped from the cell, and with a cry of relief Roddy swung to the iron door upon the turnkey and locked it. The act seemed to reassure the older man, and as the glare of the lanterns in the corridor fell upon Roddy's face the eyes of the General lit with hope and excitement. With a cry of remorse he held out the revolver.

"I was waiting to die," he said. "Can you forgive me?"

"Can you run?" was Roddy's answer.

With the joyful laugh of a boy, the General turned and, refusing Roddy's arm, ran with him down the corridor. When he saw the fallen grating he gave a cry of pleasure, and at the sight of the breach in the wall he exclaimed in delight.

"It is good!" he cried. "It is well done."

Roddy had picked up the turnkey's lantern and had given it to General Rojas. Lowering it before him, the old soldier nimbly scaled the mass of fallen masonry, and with an excited, breathless sigh plunged into the tunnel.

As he did so, in his eyes there flashed a circle of light; in his ears there sounded a cry, in its joy savage, exultant, ringing high above the tumult of the battle. The light that had blinded him fell clattering to the stones; in the darkness he felt himself held helpless, in strong, young arms.

"Father!" sobbed the voice of a girl. "Father!"

Like a coach on the side-lines, like a slave-driver plying his whip, Roddy, with words of scorn, of entreaty, of encouragement, lashed them on toward the mouth of the tunnel and, through the laurel, to the launch. Acting as rear-guard, with a gun in his hand he ran back to see they were not pursued, or to forestall an ambush skirmished in advance. Sometimes he gave an arm to Vicenti, sometimes to the General; at all times he turned upon them an incessant torrent of abuse and appeal.

"Only a minute longer," he begged, "only a few yards further. Don't let them catch us in the last inning! Don't let them take it from you in the stretch! Only a few strokes more, boys," he cried frantically, "and I'll let you break training. Now, then, all of you! Run! Run!"

Not until they were safely seated in the launch, and her head was pointed to the open sea, did he relax his vigilance, or share in their rejoicing.

But when the boat sped forward and the shore sank into darkness he heaved a happy, grateful sigh.

"If you've left anything in that flask, Vicenti," he said, "I would like to drink to the family of Rojas."

The duel between the city and the fort had ceased. On the man-of-war and on the ramparts of the fortress the guns were silent. From the city came a confusion of shouts and cheers. In his excitement, Roddy stood upright.

"It sounds as though you had won, sir!" he cried.

"Or that they have exhausted their ammunition!" answered the General. The answer was not long in coming.

From the deck of the gun-boat there sprang

THE WHITE MICE

into the darkness the pointing finger of a searchlight. It swept the wharves, showing them black with people; it moved between the custom-house and the fort, and disclosed the waters of the harbor alive with boats, loaded to the gunwale with armed men. Along the ramparts of the fort the shaft of light crept slowly, feeling its way, until it reached the flag-staff. There it remained, stationary, pointing. From the halyards there drooped a long, white cloth.

With a cheer, Roddy spun the wheel, and swung the bow of the launch toward Miramar.

"You needn't go to Curaçao to-night, General!" he cried. "This city votes solid for Rojas!"

From the wharves to the farthest limits of the town the cheers of victory swept in a tidal wave of sound. With one accord the people, leaping, shouting, dancing, and cheering, raced into the Alameda.

"To Miramar," they shrieked, "to Miramar! *Viva Rojas!*"

To those in the launch the cheers of triumph carried clearly. The intoxication of the multitude was contagious.

"What do you wish?" demanded Roddy breathlessly—"to show yourself to the people, or——"

"No!" cried the General, "to my home, to my home!"

When San Carlos surrendered, those in charge of the *cartel*, making a virtue of what they knew would soon be a necessity, threw open the cells of the political prisoners, and Peter, McKildrick, and Pedro found themselves in the street, once more free men. There they learned that Vega and his band had been routed, and that Vega, driven back to the harbor, had taken refuge on a sailing boat, and was on his way to Curaçao.

From Caracas the news was of more momentous interest. The rising of the Rojas party in Porto Cabello had led the same faction at the capital to proclaim itself in revolt. They found themselves unopposed. By regiments the government troops had deserted to the standard of Rojas, and Alvarez, in open flight, had reached his yacht, at La Guayra, and was steaming toward Trinidad. Already a deputation had started for Porto Cabello to conduct Rojas to the capital. But as to whether in freeing Rojas Roddy had succeeded or failed, or whether Rojas had been assassinated, or had been set at liberty by his victorious followers, they could learn nothing.

Only at the home of Señora Rojas could they hear the truth. Accordingly, with the rest of

THE WHITE MICE

the city, they ran to Miramar. The house was ablaze with lights, and the Alameda in front of it, the gardens, even the long portico were packed with a mad mob of people. Climbing to the railings and to the steps of the house itself, men prominent in the life of the city called for "*Vivas*" for the new President, for Señora Rojas, for the Rojas revolution. Below them, those who had been wounded in the fight just over were lifted high on the shoulders of the mob, and in it, struggling for a foothold, were many women, their cheeks wet with tears, their cries of rejoicing more frantic even than those of the men.

For a mad quarter of an hour the crowd increased in numbers, the shouting in vehemence; and then, suddenly, there fell a shocked and uneasy silence. Men whispered together fearfully. In the eyes of all were looks of doubt and dismay. From man to man swept the awful rumor that at San Carlos, Rojas had not been found.

It was whispered that, from the fortress, messengers had brought the evil tidings. The worst had come to pass. At the last moment the defenders of San Carlos had cheated them of their victory. Rojas had been assassinated, and his body thrown to the harbor sharks.

THE WHITE MICE

From the mob rose a great, moaning cry, to be instantly drowned in yells of rage and execration. A leader of the Rojas party leaped to the steps of the portico. "Their lives for his!" he shrieked. "Death to his murderers! To the fortress!"

Calling for vengeance, those in the garden surged toward the gates; but an uncertain yell from the mob in the street halted them. They turned and saw upon the balcony above the portico the figure of Señora Rojas. With one arm raised, she commanded silence; with the other, she pointed to the long window through which she had just appeared. Advancing toward the edge of the balcony, the mob saw two young girls leading between them, erect and soldierly, a little, gray-haired man.

Amazed, almost in terror, as though it looked on one returning from the grave, for an instant there was silence. And then men shrieked and sobbed, and the night was rent with their exultant yell of welcome.

With their backs pressed against the railings of the garden, Peter and McKildrick looked up at the figures on the balcony with eyes that saw but dimly.

"So Roddy got away with it," said Peter. "Pino Vega, please write! *Viva* the White Mice!"

THE WHITE MICE

With a voice that shook suspiciously, McKildrick protested.

"Let's get out of this," he said, "or I shall start singing the doxology."

An hour later, alone on the flat roof of Miramar, leaning on the parapet, were two young people. Above them were the blue-black sky and white stars of the tropics; from below rose the happy cheers of the mob and the jubilant strains of a triumphant march.

"To-morrow," said Roddy, "I am going to ask your father a favor. I am going to ask him for the use of two hours of the cell he last occupied."

"And why?" protested Inez.

"I want it for a friend," said Roddy. "Pedro tells me my friend is the man who sent word to San Carlos to have the White Mice locked up and your father moved into another cell. I want the new Commandante to lock my friend in that cell, and to tell him he is to remain there the rest of his natural life. Two hours later, the White Mice will visit him, and will smile on him through the bars. Then I'll unlock the door, and give him his 'passage-money home and a month's wages.' His name is Caldwell."

"I had no idea you were so vindictive," said Inez.

THE WHITE MICE

"It is rather," said Roddy, "a sense of humor. It makes the punishment fit the crime."

He turned, and drawing closer, looked at her wistfully, appealingly.

"Your father," he whispered, "is free."

The girl drew a long breath of happiness.

"Yes," she sighed.

"I repeat," whispered Roddy, "your father is free."

"I don't understand," answered the girl softly.

"Have you forgotten!" cried Roddy. "You forbade me to tell you that I loved you until he was free."

Inez looked up at him, and the light of the stars fell in her eyes.

"What will you tell me?" she whispered.

"I will tell you," said Roddy, "the name of a girl who is going to be kissed in one second."

THE END

DISCARDED

BETHANY
COLLEGE
LIBRARY